J. California Cooper

WILD STARS
SEEKING
MIDNIGHT SUNS

J. California Cooper is the author of the novels *Some People, Some Other Place*; *Family*; and *In Search of Satisfaction*, and of seven short story collections: *Homemade Love*, the winner of the 1989 American Book Award; *A Piece of Mine*; *The Future Has a Past*; *Some Love, Some Pain, Sometime*; *The Matter Is Life*; and *Some Soul to Keep*. She is also the author of seventeen plays and has been honored as Black Playwright of the Year. She lives in Oregon.

Some People, Some Other Place

The Future Has a Past

The Wake of the Wind

Homemade Love

Some Soul to Keep

Some Love, Some Pain, Sometime

In Search of Satisfaction

Family

The Matter Is Life

A Piece of Mine

WILD STARS

SEEKING

MIDNIGHT SUNS

———— Stories ————

WILD STARS

SEEKING

MIDNIGHT SUNS

J. California Cooper

ANCHOR BOOKS

A DIVISION OF RANDOM HOUSE, INC.

NEW YORK

FIRST ANCHOR BOOKS EDITION, APRIL 2007

Copyright © 2006 by J. California Cooper

All rights reserved. Published in the United States by Anchor Books,
a division of Random House, Inc., New York, and in Canada by
Random House of Canada Limited, Toronto. Originally published in
hardcover in the United States by Doubleday, a division of
Random House, Inc., New York, in 2004.

Anchor Books and colophon are registered trademarks of
Random House, Inc.

Cataloging-in-Publication Data is on file at the Library of Congress.

Anchor ISBN: 978-1-4000-7568-3

Book design by Donna Sinisgalli

www.anchorbooks.com

Dedicated with Love

Joseph C. and Maxine R. Cooper, my parents
Paris A. Williams, my chile

Acknowledgments

I am a very blessed person to have Janet Hill as my editor. She is brilliant as well as understanding and kind, with a diamond-bright intelligence.

I am also grateful and blessed to have Russell Perreault as my PR person with his caring and astute observation, humor, and beneficial thinking.

I thank everyone at Doubleday for everything they do for me. I truly do appreciate all of you. Tracy Jacobs, you are at the top of the list.

I thank Sharon Elise because whatever you do, I am always improved with your input.

I thank Stephen Rubin for his superlative, generous consideration for all those in his departments. He certainly contributes to the high standard Doubleday has maintained over many years.

To my readers, I can only say, from the bottom of my heart (and it is deep), I love you, I love you, I appreciate you. I respect you; which is why I write as I do. May Jehovah bless you.

Author's Note

Dear Reader,

Since I was a small child, before I could write, I have been telling stories. I was able to talk with my characters, first in the form of pets and trees then in the form of paper dolls. When I put the paper dolls away my imagination and the characters did not stop coming, producing. I love them.

I always loved to read about everything long enough to know if it really interests me. My mind absorbed the life around me; everything living. My imagination seemed to reflect things in the world around me; not just next door or a few blocks or miles away. I am blessed that my mind appreciated places far, far away. A gift from history and fairy tales, I guess.

I love humor . . . and pathos, drama, everything that is life. But there is not much humor in the world today. There is so much pain, so many mistakes being made by so many people. Many of their choices affect us. As I have said before, you can stand stark raving still and life will still happen to you.

Some of the stories in this book reflect the pain, confusion, ignorance, frustration, and emptiness crashing throughout the world today. I am reading a new book, *The Sociopath Next Door*, not because I like morbid and frightening things, but because a sociopath lives next door to a lot of people all over the world today. Apparently they are everywhere; in government, churches, schools, anywhere you can think of. If you think I am being too intense about it, just look at the condition the whole world is in.

This book does not talk about the worst things in this world. They are too painful, because I live what I write as I write. These are just a few problems people have. They may not be your problems today, thank God, but even worse ones are out there, all around us.

I would rather make you laugh and be happy. But I am always saying "Think!" Be careful with your life and your choices. So as the stories came, I wrote them. I have to blush for a few of them (and I don't blush at life easily). Because the Bible told me what was out there. Just listen, four people mentioned in the Bible were in the Garden of Eden. Three were liars, one was a murderer, and the innocent one died. We are way more crowded than Eden now.

I reach out to all of you, but *especially* to the young, the inexperienced who DO want to know a little about life without having to live some of the particulars in this book. A word to the wise can be critically important.

Wild Stars do not have to be bad stars. Some of these stars were just unwise. But that is what I often write about; people's problems, their choices. The quality of the life we make for ourselves.

Wild Stars Seeking Midnight Suns. There are billions of

stars; there is only one sun. How many wild stars do not find their sun?

I know we all stand alone in this life. Ultimately alone. We have to depend on ourselves to protect ourselves, and knowledge is our armor. I love knowledge and wisdom (they are separate). I hold on to it fiercely. The Bible says the heart is treacherous; your own heart in your own life; whom you may love, whom you may hate, your friends, the people you vote for, it goes on and on.

Freedom is expensive. Your choices can cost you your life. I don't want you to go around frightened; I would like you to go around aware. So this book may not be for people who just want to laugh, but it is for those who really care about what is going on in this nation, in this sad and lonely, desperate world. I prefer to speak of beauty and love. I prefer laughter and will be glad to get back to more of it. But I try to speak the truth in every book. There are so many soothing lies in the world already.

This book is not enough. A few stories can never tell it all. But I send this book out to you anyway, with my love. I mean that! God bless you.

$\mathcal{C}ontents$

As Time Goes By

This *story happened* in this small town to a friend of mine named Futila Ways. The people here are the same as any people in any small middlin town anywhere in America, or the world, for that matter. There's a'many of them. Maybe a little poorer than some, with many things less accessible than in large cities.

There are churches galore and a few schools, clothing stores of the cheaper variety. People who happened to have money could afford to go to better places to shop. Womens here have to look out of town for a husband, sometimes, cause you can get sick of the people you grow up with. But, after all, it was a nice, quiet, clean, boring little place.

The town must'a had promising beginnings a long time ago. Large landowners had built large proud houses on their land. But, now, over a hundred years or so, their descendants had sold off most of the land to small developers in this part of the town.

A few of the large houses remained and several rows of small houses had crept up to them.

Futila's family lived in one of the old, but neat little houses sitting in a row on Coulda Street with a younger sister, Willa, an older brother, Eddy Jr., a domestic-working mother, and a father who was a labor-mechanic at a gas station. He just kept the tools in order in the right places, didn't do much mechanic work on cars. He did his work well and kept a job so they had the bare necessities of life.

Mr. Ways (he doesn't know where his grandfather got that name from) did not have a sensitive turn of mind so he cut down the big, grand black-oak tree, and another tall beautiful tree I don't know the name of, in the front yard so he wouldn't have to rake leaves, umph umph. Then he covered the ground with cement so he wouldn't have to mow it. Just removed all the beauty and close bird songs. He wanted to do the backyard also, but his wife stopped him; she said she wanted to have a patch of land to plant a kitchen garden.

Mrs. Ways was tired and weary. Besides her regular working jobs she took care of her mother, Gramma, who suffered lifelong ills because she had struggled through the struggles. She was old and had even known people who had been slaves.

In this house Futila tried to dream about a future, her future, on hot sweaty summer nights as she threw off the damp sheet, or cold wintry nights as she pulled the wash-worn, threadbare blanket high around her neck. She was trying to see in the dark, beyond her here and now, to when and if. Just like most any poor girl anywhere in the world.

Her grandmother, sighting her grandchild staring off in some space, always talked about education. "Get that education, child, and be about thinkin your way out of here. Don't, and you gonna end up like me and your mama. Stead'a taken what you want, you gonna have to take what you can get! Where your books?! Get them books and bring em in here and teach me what you learnin in that school. Maybe I can learn somethin and get outta all this misery my own self!"

Futila loved her gramma, but didn't think Gramma knew anything about life. She would answer, "Ain't got no books! Just got some little notes I done made when the teacher was talkin."

Gramma, sitting in her rocker chair, would hit the floor hard with her knotty cane. "Bring them notes then, girl! Learn me somethin! Your sister, Willa, have books so why don't you? Put somethin in your fool-head sides of them boys!" Gramma knew her grandchild.

It was true; Futila dreamed of boys a lot. She was fourteen going on fifteen years old; her body was developing on time as it was supposed to. Had shoulder-length hair she was always fooling with, keeping it neat and near-styled. She had to wash her own clothes when the old washing machine didn't work so her clothes were not dirty, but not clean either. "Oh," she thought, "I just got such a hard time to make my future out of. I ain't never gonna get to be nobody." Then she would daydream in her classes about the man-boy. "I'm gonna marry and he gonna take me way from here. He gonna work and buy me whatever I need and want! I'll help em. I'll work too! But not like my mama works. No domestic for me! Please, God, let him come soon!"

Younger sister Willa played on the junior basketball team (when they had a basketball) and volleyball team (when they had a volleyball). She was an active young lady. She didn't study hard because she thought she didn't like to read, but she made good grades anyway. She had to, because her friend Martha, a Jewish girl who lived in one of the grand decaying old houses up Coulda Street a ways, always made good grades.

Mrs. Ways worked for Martha's father taking care of the house and cooking for Martha. Martha's mother was dead and her father was often gone on some surveying job somewhere. There was many interesting things to do there, drawing tables, telescopes, microscopes, and books, books, books. Oh, all kind'a things for little girls to do. Martha wanted to be a scientist but knew her father's money was not so great all the time. She still studied hard anyway, even at such an early age, so she could get scholarships for college someday.

Willa told Martha, "You gonna have to study the rest of your life to be a scientist! That's too much for me. I don't know what I want'a do, but I'm ready to try to do it. I sure ain't gonna stay in this place and marry none of these knuckle-head boys round here!" Willa really liked her friend Martha and was often at her house whether her own mother was there or not. There were so many interesting things to do!

Martha was not a wild child, but her interest was in wild things, insects, plants, trees, and the like. They spent much of their time outside on the land that stretched all around. Willa followed Martha around. Sometimes they even crept out in the nights to study stars with the little worn telescope Martha's father had given her. Searching and collecting, studying, until Willa developed such an interest she began to find things to collect even when she wasn't with Martha.

Futila told Willa, "You all must be crazy! Walkin round in the dark with all them snakes out there! Lookin up at the sky like a fool!" Then she would smugly return to her thoughts of boys.

Futila was as popular as most girls at school because she had sizable breasts. The man-boy she dreamed of didn't show up to carry her away so, obviously, he wasn't at her school or anywhere in town.

A year or so passed as Martha worked hard on her scholarship, still planning to go to college. And now Willa had buckled down to study because she wanted to go to college; any college. Martha said to her, "No . . . You have to choose a college that excels at what you want to study, then you know you will learn what you need to know to be able to do what you want to do. Since we both want the same things you ought to try to come where I am going." So they were both working hard on their scholarships. Martha's dad provided them with extra reference books and catalogues from universities. Martha kept her specimens in drawers and long shelves; Willa kept hers in odd boxes she was able to find, under her bed.

Futila scoffed at them, laughingly teased Willa. "You ain't gonna be no scientist or nothing. You just copyin that ole white girl, Martha, and she gonna leave you in the dust cause you can't go where she go!"

That was when Willa hitched her dream to a moving star and started doing jobs to save money. She baby-sat, washed clothes, weeded gardens, cleaned some houses, and saved every dime. When there was time from working and her studies, she and Martha continued their searches for things to study in any pasture full of trees and "wild" things.

Gramma always took a few dollars from her little government check to divide among her grandchildren. Now she gave Futila only a third as much money as before, and added the rest to Willa's share. She didn't take from Eddy Jr. "He a man," she said without explanation.

Mr. Ways wanted to help Willa, he liked what she was trying to do, but couldn't spread his money any further than it was already spread. He began splitting firewood logs for people after his regular job. He added that money to Willa's savings. He wanted to see his children "get somewhere" in their lives. After two months of this he pulled muscles in his back and could no longer do even his regular job at the filling station unless it was lying under the automobile with his back flat.

Mrs. Ways tried to interest Futila in the excitement of Willa going to college. "What are you gonna do with yourself, sister? Don't you want to make some kind'a plan for your life? You see what I'm doin and how Papa and me are struggling round here.

You not even gettin good grades in school. When you get grown and graduate from that school, we not gonna take care of you. We tired. We need some rest. Your sister is tryin to help herself. You betta try to do somethin to help yourself, too!"

Futila waved the words away, saying, "You ain't got to worry bout me. I'm a have a plan. Willa ain't so smart noway. She just follow whatever that white girl do!"

As she walked away with an armload of folded clothes, Mrs. Ways said, "She usin her own brain and everything she learn is hers. She ain't followin no fool, and she doin what SHE wants to do. If she get to that college and get a certificate and a job, her checks is gonna have HER name on em, not nobody else's, Miss Smartbutt!"

After graduation from high school Martha got her first scholarship and was sent away for higher learning to college. Willa hated to see her friend leave, and wished she had studied even harder than she had. But she kept saving even more of her money. She did without everything but pencils and paper. Letters came from Martha often, filled with references to their favorite subjects. Willa would take her letters into whatever room was empty and read them, over and over.

One day a letter came saying Martha had found a job for Willa where she could make and save more money. "And you can stay at our place here and do light housework to help costs. You are not a charity case (smile) because you can take a few classes at college until you are ready to enter a full schedule. Scholarship information is more abundant here, too."

Now, before she left her home Willa told her gramma, "Keep your money for yourself or for Eddy Jr. in case he wants to do better." She told her mother, "You gave me my brain, now I'm gonna see how good it works." She kissed her father, saying, "You take care yourself because one day I may have a job that can help you like you helped me, Papa." Willa packed her few clothes in a nice cardboard box she had painted pale green to hide the grocery advertisement on it, then she left almost immediately.

Futila was supposed to graduate the following semester, but she was stumbling through. School was not important to her except for sports events she loved to attend because, then, so many new boys from other schools came to her town. At one of the basketball games she attended she saw Dante Perks for the first time. He was tall, lean, and handsome with a bright smile in his golden-brown face topped with a dark curly natural. The sun flew out of his smile and landed smack into Futila's heart and lit up her little life!

Now Futila was a good-looking sixteen-year-old with a well-rounded attractive body. After she caught sight of him, she stared at him, smiling, all evening. She liked the way he moved as he jumped, and shook his arms and hands, for or against a score made. He looked her over also, but he looked all the girls over. Before he left to return to his little town, they talked in passing. He didn't ask her for her phone number, there were so many nice-looking girls smiling at him. But Futila made sure she had a schedule of all the games and when the next one was due. When the next game came up from his school, she was there! Her pretty dark eyes darted around looking for him.

Futila found Dante at half-time and placed herself in his vicinity. Dante was watching her watch him. He was flattered and soon they talked, flirting. He couldn't talk long because his regular girlfriend was there, watching him also. When Futila and Dante parted, he had the phone number she had grinned and slipped him. She insisted on having his. He told her, "I can't write it down now." She answered, "Just say it, I'll remember." So he did and she did. Her little heart just dreamed and dreamed and dreamed about that boy all her way home. "Dante . . . Dante . . . Dante." Music to her whole young untried mind and body.

Futila was in ninth heaven until two days passed and Dante didn't call. She made her first excuse for him, "He must'a lost that paper I gave him." So she called him. He sounded glad to hear from her and they made plans to meet on the next weekend. He missed that date, but kept the next one. In time, they became close, spending some time together, when he could get away from his studies, his family, his job, whatever. Oh, her heart was so full of joy.

Dante did like Futila. He told his friends, "She built, man! She so soft and smell so good; like vanilla cake!" Sex is mostly on all young men's minds in high school and, of course, sex entered into their relationship. She thought it would make their relationship closer, better. Well, of course, he told her it would. I mean, what else would he say? Of course.

Futila was a virgin and Dante liked being the "only" one. "I was the first and only!" he bragged to his friends.

Now, Dante didn't know much about sex his own self. He got all he could when he could. After the first triumph of "gettin" Futila had worn off, he wanted more from her. And Futila had, somehow, let him know she would do whatever he wanted her to do just to keep him. She should'a never let him know she loved him more than she loved herself!

Dante had never experienced oral sex before, he had only heard about it. He wanted to experiment with Futila. He didn't ask any other girl he was dating, cause at that time people thought that was a low-down thing to do. But he knew Futila loved him, and would try to please him.

One evening, in the back of his used secondhand car, as he held her in his arms, he said to her, "You know what, darlin? I been learning a few things from my friends."

With her head resting on his shoulder, in the darkness of the old car, she smiled up at him. "What, my love?" (She heard that in some romantic movie. In reality that's what she was living in her mind, a romantic movie.)

He smiled and took a deep breath before he said, "I learned that when a girl loves them, they will kiss them all over their body to show them how much they love them."

Still smiling, she said, "Well, I know you already know I love you."

"Yea, but you don't kiss me all over my body like their girls do."

She raised her head to see him better, "Sure I do. I kiss your chest, your back. Your body." She sighed in her self-satisfaction, and laid her head back down on his shoulder.

He put her hand on his private place, down there. "This is my body, too."

She raised her head up farther this time. "What you talkin bout?"

"If you really loved me, you would kiss me all over." He pressed her hand closer, if possible. "Here too. Just like them other girls do to their man."

Futila sat up and pulled away from him, saying, "Baby, you want me to put my . . . mouth on somethin' you pee-pee with? Baby, that ain't clean."

He shifted his shoulder away from her, a little. "What you mean, it ain't clean?! I'm clean. I bathe all the time, every day. And even if I happen to miss a spot, it's still me."

"You don't really want ME to do that, Dante. That ain't good. That ain't right."

"Who says? If it's what I want, it's right. And that is what I want, so I can know you love me." He removed his arm from around her shoulders. "And if you don't love me that much, then you don't love me at all! We can just go on home now." He leaned to start the engine up, even turned the key. "I thought I had me somebody that loved me. Hell, I ain't got nobody. I better go on home and wait for the woman to come along that is going to love me right!"

Now if Futila had stuck to her first thought and waited, or

even asked him to prove to her he loved her by not asking her that favor, she would have learned that Dante was not going anywhere. Sex was easy to get, but it was not *that* easy to get and he wanted to keep what he had. Or, she might have thought that if a person has to do something that person doesn't want to do, *to keep some-body*, maybe they are not worth keeping. Maybe they don't love you for yourself. Maybe they only want you for what they want you to do. She should'a asked him to do it to her first!

Anyway, she didn't stick to her thoughts. She didn't think at all. She did what he asked! Was a mistake! She should'a waited until they got married at least. Between husband and wife might be different. Between just somebody you know and yourself, it's too personal, too intimate for just anyone. Your body shouldn't be the friendly dump. Once you do it, you are gonna have to keep doin it cause they have found out how to handle your mind.

When her little head was bobbing around in the pit of his lap he looked down on her head, and lost a lotta respect for Fu-tila. Somehow, though he didn't understand it, he felt a little shame for himself and her. But when it felt good to him, he for-got about her, he didn't stop her. The last thing she saw on his face that night was a grin. She kissed him good night and he chastely kissed her back. He didn't want his tongue in her mouth. He thought of what she had done, and now, her lips were "nasty" to him.

The following days she waited for his call and it didn't come. He knew she would call. And she did, at least ten times a day. She annoyed his family. They didn't know everything but they laughed about her among themselves. Since she was not really important in his mind, except sexually, eventually he forgot his disdain of her. And since he had liked her, and he liked the good feelings she had given him (he had not dared ask any other girl . . . yet), eventually he answered her calls. They continued their relationship, such as it was.

Dante had been working as a mailroom clerk and stockboy to save money to help his parents send him to college. He was smart in school. He was excited to be going away. He liked Futila, but she never crossed his mind when he thought about going away because he knew she would be wherever he left her when he came back. IF he came back. If she wasn't there, so what? "Man! The cream of the crop will be at that college! I'll be in heaven!" he grinned as he told his friends.

Willa wrote one letter for all her family to her mother. She was still working, saving money. "But," she wrote excitedly, "I'm taking the basic classes I need. Algebra, geometry (ugh), chemistry and botany, right along with Martha. I do a few chores at Martha's house where I live in the only extra room; the maid's room (we can't afford a maid). It is clean and the food is wholesome and Martha's father is really kind. They bought me clothes to wear to school. I can go to seminars and listen to professors talk about science, medicine, politics, oh, everything. My life is moving slow, but steady."

Dante finally left, going about three hundred miles away, to a small business college. His family didn't have a lot of money so his father encouraged him in business administration and accounting. Futila was miserable the moment he left. He returned home for short visits on holidays, but Futila didn't always get to see him. "Family stuff," he said on the telephone. But she was happy whenever she did get to see him. They made sex quickly in uncomfortable places, if they made it at all.

Futila was jealous of his going to college and leaving her working behind a counter at the drugstore. She blamed him! She was so glad to be able to say, "My sister is in the East going to college." At least, that put her somewhere in the vicinity of college. Dante always answered, "That isn't you."

Time passed quickly for Willa. Soon she wrote home, "I'm taking classes in French, biology, and studying a little Greek with Martha. Martha's father has set up a small laboratory for us in the house, including microscopes and shelves for our many books." Willa and Martha were passionate in their quest for learning, for their degrees. Both needed another scholarship.

Futila didn't feel balanced in her life; something was wrong. She didn't feel good about life anymore. She was trying to make up her mind to quit Dante or something. She didn't feel loved. She hated that "mouth" thing, but that's what he insisted on now when she did get to see him. Sometimes he didn't even have sex with her the normal way. "Oh, Lord," she thought, "I have so many things to decide. Why did you give me this life, Lord? Everybody is better off than me!" But she still ate, slept, and dreamed "Dante." He seldom gave her a thought until she called him, charging it on her parents' phone. And she called him often. Too often. He, just as often, lied, telling people, "Tell her I'm not here!"

Dante finished his second year of college, which he had loved. It was full of women, but he had managed to keep his grades up. Now, he had been working, a year or so, as accountant in an insurance office. In college, during his early loneliness, he had started out writing Futila a note once a week. She wrote seven times a week and worried her mother for the stamps. In time, several weeks would pass and she didn't hear from Dante at all. She would rush to the mailbox every day and find nothing for her there.

When he didn't come home to her after he received his BA degree, she couldn't understand. When she pleaded with him and failed to get him to return, she said, "Well, I'll come find a job there! I want to be with you! We b'long together, Dante."

Thinking of his social life, he discouraged her mightily. "No, no, you don't want to come here. You can't come here. I don't want you here. You will distract me, and I need to concentrate."

Futila was not a dumb girl, she simply just applied her mind to her future with boys, and Dante, and not to her own future with herself. At least she was holding on to the same job she had started with, though she still lived at home with her struggling parents.

Willa had driven herself near illness studying and working to acquire money and grants to finish her master's degree. When her finals were at last completed she slept for three days, only waking to eat. She and her friend rejoiced when a job she and Martha had applied for in Egypt was approved with Willa as a co-worker. Their dreams were beginning to come true!

It was about this time, after one of Dante's trips home to see his parents, that Futila discovered she was pregnant. She was elated! Happily she wrote to Dante because she couldn't get him on the phone. (Her mother kept the phone locked because Futila ran the bill up too much for their budget and Futila didn't want to pay her share.)

Dante called her immediately after receiving her letter. He screamed at her, "I can't come home! This is my home now! I can't have no baby now! I don't want no baby! I'm not going to mess my life up! And I won't get married. I . . . I can't marry you, Futila! I don't want to. And, another thing, that baby ain't mine! You must'a slept with everybody in town by now. Don't put this off on me."

When Futila finished crying she told her parents and they involved Dante's parents. His mother said, "She is trying to trap my son!" (Futila had dabbled a little with other boys.) Her mother said, "We can't afford to take care your son's mistakes." His father said, "I'll get the law on them. We'll see whose baby this little tramp is blaming on my son!" In the end, a hasty marriage was arranged. Futila was happy. "I got my man. I'm a married woman. My future is here at last." Dante was not happy, his thoughts were different. "I got a burden. My future is over."

After the marriage, Dante's father made him come home, get a job, and stand by his child. Dante was smart in his field, and got a job with no problem, although he did it in a cloud of anger and rage. He began to seriously compare his wife, her education and sensibilities and style, to the women he was leaving behind, the women with education and promise.

Passing over all the petty arguments, the young couple managed to have some agreeable times together. Futila was still attractive and he still liked her. It was agreeable to Dante having a piece of lovemaking right beside him every night. Then . . . the baby was born and dirty diapers, 2 a.m. and 4 a.m. feedings and crying noises interrupted his life every day and night. Oh, all the things that happen in a new-baby household.

Dante began to stay away from home more, and even out late at night till early in the morning. As a sophisticated college man, he was very popular with the young ladies in the small town. He had a nice car and wore his old college clothes when he relaxed, and stylish suits to work. He went into the insurance business as an employee and did tax returns on the side for a few years. Then he opened his own business. Insurance did so well, he kept only the largest tax customers and concentrated on insurance. He prospered.

His wife, Futila, had another child and gave up her countergirl job. She stayed at home being a housewife and mother. He continued to prosper. She was proud of that, among her friends, at first. Then, in a few years of changing diapers, cooking for herself (he didn't always come home to eat), preparing baby food, she realized that her husband was free. Free of her.

Free! In his own private office, with telephone, new car, and uncounted money; he was free. She was surrounded with the washing, housecleaning, grocery shopping, a dumb TV, two small children, and friends she had thought were jealous of her. She also thought her husband could be sleeping with her friends. They looked satisfied, while she wasn't satisfied at all.

She knew, by now, he had other women. Sometimes they called her house. Figuratively speaking, she began to lose her mind. Her life became bitter to her. What good is love that no one shares?

She thought of God, but didn't know much about God. Her parents had been too tired for church. Gramma knew God, but couldn't get anyone to take her to church, and her grandchildren didn't want to hear the stuff she talked about anyway. She was too old to know anything.

So Futila didn't know how to pray. But she was learning; sometimes in the middle of the night in an empty bed.

Futila was young, attractive, but she didn't feel good. Dante was always on her mind, but out of her sight. She argued with him, but what could she do? He told her, "You can leave." She didn't want to give up her place in his life. She had nothing to turn to, except that job as a countergirl at the drugstore. And Time was going by.

Dante did love his children, they looked just like him. That was a good thing because it made it easier for his parents to accept them. His parents loved their grandchildren so he never thought of leaving Futila. Why should he? He was doing whatever he wanted to do anyway.

———

Now that she could afford it Futila bought pretty nightgowns, sexy perfume, and had regular hair care. Money don't buy love, chile. Those things barely bought her moments. But, you know, there are times when you turn over and your spouse is beside you smiling, warm and cozy, and things just happen. But Futila wasn't smiling; that took the "cozy" out. So the intimate moments became fewer. And Time was passing by.

But she loved Dante and there was no her without him. Life was a zero. No party or gathering was fun. No holiday dreams were made. They seldom made love anymore. She had to play with him while he slept, then crawl on top of him when he, inadvertently, became "ready," and make love to herself. Sometimes his body didn't respond; he had had sex with someone else too recently. Time was going by at a steady pace, as usual. Several years passed that way.

Willa had been home several times to see her parents and bring them things from different places in the world. She had her Ph.D. in biochemistry, just as Martha had, and she was now Dr. Willa Ways. She had worked projects in Africa, Greece, and Peru, among other countries. She had even written two books.

Willa had her own condominium in New York and her own bank accounts. She had thought of marriage several times: doctors, leaders in the field of science. She was quite attractive to several men. "But I really want to do a few more things before I marry. Besides, I'm not in love and I want to love the man I marry. He won't have to be a doctor of anything, I can afford to support my husband, if I have to," she would laugh. But she kept putting marriage off, thinking, "I have time." Time was passing, but in her life she had already used it wisely, so it didn't hurt as it passed.

Futila had begun following her husband in the car he had bought her, parking it in strange hidden places she thought he would not see. She watched his office to see who went in, came out, and when he left. Most of the time he knew she was out there watching him. His co-workers and employees laughed at her. A few women didn't laugh at her, they felt sad for her. They understood the pain.

Futila didn't want a divorce. Now, she just wanted to prove to him he was a liar and he was cheating on her. Why she had to prove it to him is a question, because he already knew it.

She listened closely when he came home and slept, whispering questions close to his ear to see if she could make him talk in his sleep. Listen to me, chile: She had hidden, lying under parked cars, crouched in scary bushes, secreted in dark, empty houses and empty lots in the darkness of night, until Dante would come out of some woman's house or some motel room.

Finally she began to confront him wherever she found him, in a loud and brazen voice no matter the early morning hours. She would forget her social standing. He would argue briefly as he angrily or nonchalantly passed her by, going to his car that was parked right in front of the woman's house, and drive away. He never hit her, just pushed her away from hitting him. When he was gone she would stand in front of whichever house it was, and call whichever lady it was, all kinds of bitches and things until she remembered her society friends would hear about it. Then outside in the street, by herself, she would run crying to her car and rush home to confront him more. This went on for years. Her grief and pain had begun to show on her face, in her body, even in the way she stood or walked. Bent. She told herself, "He's gettin older. He gonna stop all this mess. He gettin old and his time is runnin out. He can't keep this up." But she was getting older also. Her time was running out also. Time was passing by, chile.

Her close friends asked her, "Why don't you leave him? Your children are almost ready for college. He will have to give you some of the property. At least your home. Pack your tears away and pack your bags, and go get yourself a education, it ain't too late! Or meet someone else who can love you and you could love back. Someone who will do you right!" But she wasn't sure what she wanted anymore. She was obsessed and confused. Well, when did she ever stop to learn anything?

Futila didn't like to hear any romantic love songs, or even see romantic people together now. Thought women were dumb to believe in such things. Thought every man was a liar. But still, she lied too. Everyone is a liar, sometimes. But some are dangerous. You're supposed to have sense enough to recognize which is which as often as possible. Then you can build your life better.

Futila always answered, "I ain't never gonna give him no divorce so he can go off with them bitches and they get what's s'posed to be mine!!" One close old friend, from the drugstore days, said, "Well, they gettin it anyway, so evidently it ain't yours. You ain't got no education and you ain't got him. Let him go! Let that man go so you can be free to find you some happiness. You killin yourself and every year that passes, you don't look as good as you did yesterday. Leave while you have a chance! God is good, chile! He made the heart be able to love more than once or twice or even three times."

But Futila held to her thoughts. "I'll never give him no divorce. I'll never give him that satisfaction! He ain't never gonna get rid of me!" And so she built her prison, and was locking her own self in!

Dante never really got to know his wife, but his sureness of her constant, constant presence had changed any passion he could have had for her long ago. You can smother love, chile. Besides, she never showed him much. Her thoughts were all about him, and so were his. That interested him, but there is more to life, even to him.

He loved "strange, new pieces" of sex. Let me tell you, I bet he had a strange piece at home in his wife he never got to.

Now, in what he thought of as his fruitful life, his drab living lay out in front of him full of sex moments and boredom, just like his past. Except for his children. His life wasn't as good as

Futila thought it was. What he was, was a lonely man looking for love all in one place: between his legs. He thought he was having fun, and maybe he was, but any fool can have some fun; why not have some sense, too.

At the same time, Futila didn't know her husband. The love Futila thought she felt for Dante long ago, was fed by wanting someone she thought others wanted. Then, in time, jealousy, jeopardy, the dread of loss, and her pride in him instead of in herself, became her life and a symbol of her love. And all that time, Time was going by. I could be wrong, but I don't think so. And I have to try to think because I am poor. Thinking is free! and it can work!

Finally one day, tired of hearing the same complaints from Futila, one of her friends told her, "Hell, Futila, you ain't gonna get what you want from Dante either. You ain't nothin but a spy; you ain't no wife, and you ain't much woman either. You ain't free from your own fears! Don't nobody know what's going to happen in their life, but don't just stand there and cry about life! do something about it!"

About that time Willa came home to visit and introduce her parents to her new husband, a doctor of anthropology with a minor in geology. He was very attentive to Willa. Futila was jealous. When they were alone, Futila told her sister, "He may be a doctor and everything, but he still ain't nothin but a man!"

Willa smiled, saying, "He can't help that. I'm glad there are men on this earth, Futila. But they are not all the same, just like women are not all the same. It was up to me to choose carefully which one I want to deal with and love. He asked me to marry him and I was free to ask, seek, pay attention to everything about him I could. To learn, as much as possible, what kind of life we might have together. I was interested in his faults first, after I grew to love him, because I wanted to know if I could live with them. I decided I could."

Futila laughed a short, ugly laugh. "That don't mean it's gonna turn out right!"

"No." Willa shook her head. "You're right. That is up to my husband and me. And when, if ever, something becomes too large for me to handle, when I am only fifty-five or sixty-five percent happy in our life, then I will not be happy enough. Then I will have to recognize my love does not mean enough to him and I will have to let him get on with the business of making his life better. Fifty-fifty is not good enough for me. I'm better off than that when I am alone. It will have to be around seventy-five percent good for us. It's not that hard to make someone happy, or satisfied, if you love them and they love you. It's the love that does the work or works the magic. We love each other and I don't think either one of us, my husband or I, is a fool. I wanted kindness, honesty, manners, and cleanliness of body, mind, and spirit, as much as possible. I've learned in all my studying. Spiritual matters are very important; they constitute the values of a person. I know we are human. But I didn't want anyone with an overstuffed ego or too much ambition or an atheist, because I want peace in my life. And my husband . . . had to love me, first. Remember, the love is the magic part of the formula. Then, when you have a good thing, you do your best to keep it."

Futila frowned. "Well, I don't care what nobody says, I ain't, am not, going to give Dante what he wants! Let him suffer!"

Willa placed her hand on her sister's bent, tired shoulder, saying, "Well . . . that is your business, Futila, but Dante obviously does not know he is suffering. But you do know you are." She turned to lock a suitcase. "Well, we have to leave the family now. We have an appointment at the Louvre in Paris."

When Futila went to her empty bed that night, as on most nights, she wept. Crying hard into her pillow as she thought, "I don't care. I ain't never gonna let that bastard get away from me and run to one of them women and give them what rightfully b'longs to me. Oh God, give me some wisdom to know what to do with this man you gave me."

But Heaven's advice was already in the Bible. "Consider carefully and choose wisely. The heart can be treacherous." I don't say the Bible says it in that way, but I know it says it.

I'll tell you this, too. It looked like Dante had the best life in this marriage, but he didn't. They were both losers. Sex is one of the keenest, greatest pleasures in life. But it has rules like everything in life has rules; you heard of the laws of nature, haven't you? When a person violates the rules of love it is as if they were stealing from themself. If a person could make a sport of sex, multiple partners and all, life might be gayer, but experience has taught a multitude of people that a lotta sex and gaiety does not make life happier. Sometimes it makes life lonelier. And you cannot have a real marriage when you break the laws of marriage. The very act, the privacy, the personal warmth, the intimacy shared with the special one in your life, cannot be topped by a million different burning moments with a person passing through your life and hands. The flame is quick, but not bright and does not burn long; there is no long sustaining warmth that goes to the bones of your body! The pleasure of sex is an inside job. It's a large part of the stuff you furnish your house of marriage with. You can't leave your furniture out in the street and expect to find it there like you left it when you return, again and again. And Time is always going by.

Love, and sex, is the bridge that two people cross, together, in a marriage. Love, the strength of that bridge, is what makes a marriage secure and good; for a true, shared satisfaction and as much happiness as you can expect in this world. Dante never took the time to have an enjoyable union . . . with anyone. Sex and money were his desires. Just sex and money was what he got. Both are good, but not half as good as Love. Both slip through your life and disappear just like Time slips through.

Futila was not happy, but, Dante was not happy, either.

I wonder if you think he was.

As for me, I know Time is going by. So now, it's time for me to go somewhere else. I've got to go; Time is passing by.

The Eye of the Beholder

The *longer I live* the more I can see how people, the world, will never have things right. They label everything so they can remember what they think. Right—wrong, black—white, too big—too little, pretty—ugly, and on and on.

I know they are trying to map their way to some satisfactory end, but if the labels are wrong, the map will be wrong. A person may not reach their destination. Or, usually, they confuse someone else.

And, that is the point.

Do you know, strange as it may seem, everybody on this earth looks good to somebody? But a person who goes by this world's lying rules can suffer a lot of pain in their life. Unnecessary pain and confusion in the heart of their soul.

Tell you what I mean. There was a good-sized family, the Kneeds, who lived in a rented house close to me. The last child born in that family was a girl named Lily Bea. Lily Bea came to be a friend of mine. I was older, but what difference does that make. The mother, Sorty Kneed, was, or had been, a good-looking woman, and all that got her was a husband she played around on, and four or five kids was all I could see she got out of it. All her children were assorted pretty, cute, and handsome, if you see what I mean. When Lily Bea was born to Sorty, she was not a "pretty" baby. No, she wasn't.

Even her own family made fun of Lily Bea. As she grew, she turned out to be really sweet, a nice child, but she remained "uncomely," as they say in the Bible. She was teased and talked about enough to know she was different. She knew she was not cute or pretty like her sisters or her peers anywhere, neighborhood, church, or school. But her sweetness and manners made her an attractive child to me. I don't know why those people, her own family, didn't seem to like that child.

Now, she wasn't the kind of ugly that made other people always laugh at her. But just ugly enough, to her, for her to try to make herself invisible when others stared a few extra moments. Her mother made her think ugly was also dumb. So Lily's thoughts were a mixture of light and dark. Outdoors, around people, her thoughts were dark.

She always placed herself in the back of any crowd, the back of any room, the back of everything, behind all eyes that should be looking the other way. She grew up a very serious young woman, very quiet. She spoke only when she was spoken to. That's a shame because she had a voice lovely to hear. A sweet, tender sound made words she spoke into a soft melody.

They told her she was built funny, too. Square. And said her face was too long, her eyes too small. But her eyes were not too wide apart or too close together, they were just not set evenly in her face. One eye, you could hardly notice it, was set just a little higher than the other.

Her mouth was not small, it had substance. The lower lip was full, the upper lip was thin. It just seemed nothing matched. Her teeth stuck out a bit, but not much, and they were even teeth and flashing white. Clean. But they teased her anyway, adding to her shame of what wasn't really anything; or something almost everybody has.

Her nose was not huge, but it was too big for her face. Her skin was a chestnut brown. All the girls in her family had a bumpy skin condition and Lily Bea's was worst of all. I told her just keep keeping it clean, see what time and Mother Nature would do. But she wouldn't have ever put any makeup on anyway. Call attention to her face!? No, Lord. She just kept it clean and used Vaseline on it till they called her "greasy-face." Then she only used the Vaseline at night.

She had a head of thick, brown hair because her mother made her keep it braided. Her arms and legs were round and slim. They called them skinny. Her hands were narrow with long fingers with a fine shape and color. Her neck and back had a fine line, which made her movements smooth. Her waist was extra small, so her hips flared, like they were supposed to. I listened to them laugh at her, but I know what looks good.

They laughed, and said she looked funny. But, I knew she was just incomplete; nature wasn't finished with her. I could see she was going to be very well built when nature was through building her. And best of all, the intelligence on her face was sunshine inside her body. But she believed them. She loved her mother, believed everything she said, whether mother was drunk or sober. She did everything her mother told her to do.

From being so quiet, she had time to do more thinking. She preferred being alone whenever it was possible. She would look off into some space and sing softly to herself in that lovely voice. She would stop singing if anybody came within hearing. I think she didn't want them to mess that pleasure up for her.

Being alone so much, she learned reading and loved books. She would read about anything and everything. Whenever you saw Lily Bea, she always had a book in her hands or under her arm. Be reading! All kinds of books. As she was growing up, we talked a lot. I learned things from her I had never thought of; didn't know enough to begin to think of them. I had got married before I finished school.

Well, time passes and things change. They didn't tease her about the same things; they found a new question. "Who you gonna find to marry you, Lily Bea?" Told her mother, Sorty, "You better get that girl some plastic surgery!" And laughed out of their own little ugly faces. Sometimes they even hugged Lily Bea, cause they didn't really hate her. They just didn't have sense enough to think about how deep those words could hurt. Deep, chile, deep.

So Lily Bea just kept separating herself from other people. Youngsters played or gossiped in the streets or the schoolyard and she went off alone, stayed in the classroom or library at school. Or alone, if chance permitted, in the bedroom she shared with her sisters. Reading or dreaming. Thinking, reading, or dreaming.

Now, you know that child, in all those years, had plenty sense enough to know she must be different. She got tired of being round her house with her family. And she got tired of people.

A piano teacher, up the street, felt sorry for Lily so she gave her piano lessons for free. She practiced alone at school.

The librarian suggested good books for her because she was just reading anything no matter what it was. The librarian was a good one and she gave Lily really good cultural and classic books to read. She read a lot of fiction, then Lily discovered and loved nonfiction. Among others, she read the biography of Coco Chanel and started learning sewing at school. School is a blessed thing. For a while Lily wanted to become a teacher. But it would take a long time, and schools were too full of people. People that might tease or laugh at you.

Her home was full of strong, and even strange, personalities. They fought, they laughed, and they stole from each other, because none had much of anything. Her mother and father had loved and fought when he was around. But laughter pervaded the house after the tears, after the pain. The laughter covered the ugliness they didn't want to recognize. Somehow Lily Bea developed a sense of humor that helped to carry her over her own pain.

Well, anyway, Lily grew up and graduated high school. Her family even found a reason to laugh at her good scholarship; said, "You so ugly you ain't got nothin to do but get good marks!"

Her father was gone, but a new man was there, off and on. So Lily stayed home to help her mother. Her sisters were all married and gone on their own. Lily wouldn't go anywhere too much in the public, so she didn't go out to get a job. She would have loved to go to college, a college where no one knew her. But college was out of the question for her.

This vexed her mother. "What am I gonna do with this grown chile layin round on me?! She is over seventeen years old! I need some money comin in this house. Ain't no welfare here! I ain't got nothin to give Lily! She got all them brains, she betta use um!"

Now . . . There was a dirty old man who had an angry leg that made him crippled, Mr. Nettles, who owned the cleaners, Clean Cleaners, a block or two away from Sorty and Lily Bea's house. He was always dragging or twisting around his shop. Sorty went over there and asked him for a job for her daughter, Lily, because she had a dress she wanted cleaned. She had intended to exchange a few hours of Lily's work for the cleaning of the dress.

The cleaning man, Mr. Maddy Nettles, had been sitting around in his shop, for years, watching women when they came in or passed by his place. Watching women and wishing for one of his own. He couldn't place Lily Bea, but he agreed to the deal.

He was hoping Lily Bea would be a good-looking woman, but when Lily Bea came to his shop, he thought her looks could make her more vulnerable to his approaches. So he gave her a little job to do, and then extended the little job to a steady job, two or three times a week. "I ain't got much money, don't make much. But you need to have some little money of your own in your own pocket, girl. You just keep this job steady and we will work things out," he said as he pinched her arm.

In time, he took to touching and feeling in almost secret places on Lily Bea. Lily Bea was raised in a family where everything was talked about at home. She was a virgin, but sex held no mystery for her. The fact that she had no money and needed a job was the fact she thought of. She let him fool around with his fingers a bit. Not much, but a bit. Her face was serious when she told him, "I don't want you to do anything that hurts me. You cannot put anything *in* me, not even your fingers."

He liked the way she talked kind'a proper. A strong desire for the young woman grew in him. Daily. He gave her more hours to work. He gave her more money; not too much, but a bit.

She was able to keep her own clothes cleaned and to spend money on better material to sew. She sewed on his machines, and bought books she could keep. They were hers, belonged to *her*.

Maddy Nettles had traveled a bit in his day. He told her about the many beauties of the earth and added to her dreams. But her dreams were taking her mind away from her little job, and she dreamed of a better job. A better place in life. Her dreams never included him or his shop.

He didn't want Lily to leave. He loved her. In his way. When he told Lily Bea, she was in a type of awe. Even at that little dry, cripple man, Maddy Nettles, anybody, loving her! She had felt other boys looking at her, many times, but she never looked back at them because she thought they were looking at her ugliness, or her skin. She thought of the money and did not answer him.

Because of her reading so many things, Lily knew of dermatologists. She saved any money she could hide from her mother so she could go to one. It took three or four visits, but in time her skin cleared. Her eyes shone with her inner joy. Maddy thought the brightness in her eyes was for him even though she still showed no interest in him. He needed to believe that. She continued saving more of her little money from her mother, saving toward some future she wasn't certain of.

Beneath all the interests she carried around in her head, Lily Bea's heart was still steeped in misery. She thought her life was desolate and would always be desolate. But, in some small ways, her life was moving on.

She had always loved dancing, ballet and modern dancing. She would never let anyone see her try to use her body (which her family told her was so strange). But she had passed a new dance studio several times, dreamed about it, and decided to use a few of her dollars and sign up for classes. She loved the lessons she was able to take. The feel of her body moving lightly to the graceful, rich, full sounds of music. In her mind she danced, at last, like the fairies in fairy-tale books she loved. She prayed, "Heavenly God, thank you." She was in the midst of another lift, a reaching, in her lonely life. Lily may have been poor, but her mind was rich. It was reaching out, branching, into something other than ugliness, anger, and poverty of spirit. She was slowly building her future.

Maddy Nettles was middling poor, but he was very skilled in cloths of many fabrics from having worked in his past on rich, luxurious passenger ships as a tailor or cleaner. He had learned from masters and his specialty was cleaning and caring for fine silks, satins, laces, and such. Over the years his reputation for such work was known and employed by the best cleaning establishments. They gave him their finest things to clean, things they did not want ruined by a novice because their customers were the rich and powerful. They didn't come down to his shop, he picked orders up. When he had done their work he delivered them, finished and fine.

He had striven long and hard in his life, acquiring an angry, crippled leg along his way. He was very tight-fisted with his money. He wanted a woman, but he loved his money and did not want a woman who would abuse his money by spending too much of it. He wanted a woman, of his own, to sleep with every night. To love.

Maddy knew Lily Bea avoided people her own age. He thought, "A young wife, like Lily, might not be a bad idea. She can't do no better noway." He decided to ask Lily to marry him.

One night, after she had gone for the day, the shop was empty and dark, he wondered, "Should I ask her mama, or should I just go on and ask her?" He rubbed his crippled leg with one hand as he thought of the marriage. "She ain't got no real home or nothin else she gonna hate to leave. Absolutely no real home whatsoever. Her mama ain't nothin to count on neither." These thoughts roiled around in his mind a week or two as he watched the young woman, then he decided to speak to her mother. "Because Lily Bea ain't got sense enough to know the best thing to do about nothing!"

Also, he knew Lily Bea might refuse him. He knew better how to handle her mother, Sorty.

The next time, soon, Sorty came in to borrow a dollar or two, he spoke to her. "You know you got a fine hardworking girl here."

Mindful of the money, and her own self-deception, she answered, "Well, I sure do my best! She all right. She do the best she can. It's a good thing she good for somethin," she laughed.

Maddy tried to laugh with Sorty, but could only smile a tight smile. "Sure is . . ." He paused. "If I could, and she wasn't so young, I'd marry her, and keep her in good condition all her life. I mean, take her off your hands and take care of her . . . right."

"Right?"

"Well, Sorty, you a busy woman with more on your mind than a young foolish girl around that you have to worry about. She at that age, she gonna get into somethin! If she was to have a good settled man, a husband, lookin out after her, you be better off."

They laughed. Together.

Sorty, thinking to herself quickly, "Lily Bea ain't ever goin to make it to no college, and ain't nobody goin to be askin her to marry up with em, cause don't nobody even ever ask her to go nowhere on a date or nothin. She might lay on me all my life, and I'm not gonna stay with that bastard I got much longer then these kids get grown, if I stay that long."

"Well, Mr. Cleanerman, you might just have you a wife. She a good girl. A sweet girl. You could do a lot worser than Lily Bea! You and me'll just have to talk a little bit more bout some things tween us. You just be thinkin bout how much you gonna be thankful to me! I'll be thinkin bout what to tell Lily Bea!"

They laughed together again.

Sorty was still laughing as she went out of his shop with a few dollars gripped tightly in her hand.

We might as well skip all the lies and chicanery these two people used on each other, unnecessarily; he wanted a woman and she wanted Lily Bea off her empty hands. The deal was struck.

Always slow to speak up for herself, and believing what her mother told her about nobody else ever wanting her, Lily Bea let her mother make her decisions. "It's for your good!" Mama said.

Lily Bea, with a confused, fearful look on her face, was married, posthaste. With tightened face, she stared down at the floor of the little parlor of a justice of the peace as he spoke the words that changed her whole life. Her mind dazed, turning, rushing, crashing into some space she would now have to hide in, anew. Sorty, her mother, stood by, tightly smiling and holding her purse that held one hundred crisp dollars as Lily became the mistress of a dingy cleaning shop with a grasping, slavering, sex-hungry husband.

"It's for that poor, ugly child's good!" Sorty thought. "I done my duty. Her damn daddy, whoever he was, ain't never done nothin for her! Maddy gonna help her, and gonna help me too! Best thing I can think of for everybody! That's the truth, Lord!" (She was even gonna try to lie to God!)

Maddy, to help matters along, bought a rabbit-fur coat from the pawnshop. He had it wrapped, special, proud of his gift. "I'm givin her a fur coat just like a rich man do. She gonna see what kind of good man she gettin!"

Lily Bea accepted the gift like the child she was, and smoothing the worn fur with her hands, thanked Maddy. She wasn't quite sure what was happening. When Maddy hugged her (at last! a chance to really put his hands on her!) she just smiled, and moved away from him as soon as she could without being impolite.

Lily Bea hadn't realized she could refuse her mother and Mr. Nettles. Her much dreamed and fantasized about wedding night was like a nightmare. Maddy hadn't had much loving except for an occasional prostitute; he hated to pay out his money, that's why it was only occasional. Famished for warm flesh on the wedding night he had, in anticipation, slavered over, his claw-hands grasped, pulled, stuck, rubbed, twisted, frantically, the young virgin body. He gave her not one thought, except to think all he put his hands on was his. "I have my own woman's body here with me every day and all night!"

On her wedding night, and for days after, Lily Bea felt pain in every place on her body where pain can find the soul of the flesh.

About a year later, when she did realize she could refuse him, she did refuse the too ardent grasp and clasp of his greedy hands and arms. Her body was frail, and sickly, and by then, her love dreams had been massacred.

Lily had nowhere to turn. Her mother needed and enjoyed the little money she could "borrow" from Mr. Cleanerman. "Chile, it can't be all that bad. That's just married life. It gets better . . . sometime. But, that's your married home now, under God." No help could be expected from her.

Lily Bea had no one to depend on but herself.

She prayed often to God, saying, among other things, "Deliver me away from this sorrow, dear God. Stay inside me, with me, so I can live through this. All my life, I've hidden myself, saved myself for something special to me. Is this it, God? This is not it, dear God. Deliver me. Please."

It was about two years into the marriage when she realized the hold her little body had on him. She used that power to refuse him. She made a pallet on the floor for herself to sleep on. Maddy Nettles ranted and raged, but Lily Bea's answer was silence. She slept on that pallet on every night she could take the rantings of her husband. They were many.

One of her excuse pleas was, "There is so much work I have to do in the shop. I have to keep the book records for our taxes. Now that I have learned to handle the silks and satins, and the laces even, my time is constantly being spread around. You deliver them, but I clean and prepare them. I keep the shop clean. Then I have to come in here and clean these rooms. I have to shop for food and other things, supplies. Then I have to cook, serve, and then, clean up again." She sighed. "I am truly tired, Maddy."

(She had called him "Mr. Nettles" until he insisted she call him "Maddy." "What will people think! My own wife calling me, 'Mr.' Can't you say 'dear' or 'sweetheart' like other wives do?")

Maddy wanted his wife in his bed. He would do, almost, anything to get her body back where he wanted it. He thought about the matter of her exhaustion for several days. "She ain't got no business bein tired! She young!" He did not want to add to his workload because his angry, crippled leg was bothering him more and more. Pain interfered with his lovemaking, when he could get it. "Troubles, troubles, all the time, Lord. No rest for the weary!"

Usually, Maddy made all deliveries to his customers because he did not think Lily Bea was good-looking enough for his customers to see her and know she was his wife. Finally, he decided to hire someone, a trusted young man, Robert, working his way through college who had done odd jobs for him in the past.

Robert Earner was a hard worker, a scuffler, a survivor. And he was a loner; he thought he was too black in color. He didn't have an inferiority complex, he thought he had a "face reality" situation. His was a good mind. He was in a small college, studying and working to lift himself out of the dire poverty of his own family. He was glad to get the steady job, even at the low wage Maddy paid. He delivered parcels to the larger cleaning establishments for the rich, which sent their fragile materials to the poor specialist, Maddy, of Clean Cleaners.

Robert had known Lily Bea in passing, but had never paid much mind to anything other than his books and learning. Maddy threw in cleaning up the shop a bit, just to get his full dollars' worth of work, and to make Lily less tired. After all, the point was to get his wife back into his bed and arms; though he told her she had funny strange legs, he wanted himself back between them.

Maddy said many things to Lily Bea, always with a little laughter, that continued to assault her feelings. He wanted her to feel "less" than he was, or even "only" as he was. He thought to hisself, "If she don't think she too much, at her age, she ain't gonna run off with the first thing comes her way! She ain't no better 'en I am! Even her mama say so."

Books were a waste to Maddy Nettles. "You ain't got no time for them books you keep bringin from that lib'ary." Oddly enough, books were what first established a rapport between Lily Bea and Robert Earner. Robert was impressed with someone else who loved books. Of course, they talked about what she was reading and what he was studying. Maddy discouraged these quick talks. "Boy, what you think you doin? Don't be wastin my wife's time, and making me pay you for it too!"

They talked less because they were not interested in each other at the time Maddy spoke to Robert. But in one of the quick moments of exchanging thoughts, Robert mentioned his college to Lily. "You know, you are learning good things from Mr. Nettles, but they have classes at the college where you can learn all about fabrics and special knowledge to make your own self mistress of this profession, if this is what you really want to do."

Lily didn't want "cleaning clothes" to be her profession, but, as she thought about it, "It would be a good excuse to have some time to myself. Time away from . . . everything. And, if this is the work I have to do, at least I can learn for myself."

She signed up for a class before she told Maddy. He wanted to get angry, but didn't know what to get angry at. He also thought, "Maybe she is coming round to knowing I am her husband and she is my helpmate, and this is our work, together. Our business." So he let her go to the college two times a week.

She studied professional cleaning and fabrics classes about six months. During that time she and Robert met at school; they talked and they liked each other. Robert, on closer look, hearing her voice, seeing the light in her eyes, feeling her touch, was falling in love with Lily. She never seemed to see his color. The beautiful color God gave some people, he thought was unattractive.

Why, she could even talk about his studies in engineering. Many times he thought to himself, "She understands!" Of course, they talked about other things. It was her first experience with a stranger, a man, in which she found enjoyment. And, while he had admired the usual pretty girl, he had never really gotten to know one. He thought Lily Bea was pretty and wondered why he had never noticed it before. "I don't like that ugly fur coat she wears, though."

She learned even more than her class taught because she took out extra books on the subject, adding to her knowledge. On her way back to work from college, she sneaked in a few minutes at the dance studio to dance a few steps, twirling alone in the welcoming rooms among welcoming people. Then she would be off, to work and her husband.

Robert and Lily Bea were very friendly at school, but back at the cleaners they were self-conscious about their friendship in front of Maddy Nettles. They felt dirty, because his thoughts were. But that seemed to push their feelings more together. Each began to feel the other's presence stronger. Sex would seem to be rearing its head a bit. But sex did not get to tremble over them; it was not what either wanted. Then.

Sex was the last thing Lily Bea wanted anything to do with, and Robert had not thought of Lily in that way before. But, now, their bodies were like a magnet. They began to avoid closeness in the little shop because, somehow, their closeness changed there. In the shop, when close, their breathing, so near each other, gave them the intensity of suffocating. Lily found it hard to breathe. If they happened to look at each other at these times, it was like a caress, a climax of a sort. It embarrassed them, even as they enjoyed the innocent goodness of the feelings.

They grew to love each other, a little. But it was not a love they chose to do anything about, except to enjoy the closeness, the feelings and sharing of thoughts. These things were new to the both of them. Lily had other plans even though she didn't know what they were. Robert wanted his life to be free, to lift himself up, and beyond his past.

Maddy Nettles noticed; their feelings became so intense, he

began to feel it. Not thinking of the help Robert was to him, Maddy took Lily out of school and fired Robert, immediately. "Boy, you get on way from here. You makin your way to breakin up my home. Naw, you get on way from round here. And don't come back neither." He took up his own chores again. His angry leg was angrier than ever, as angry as he himself was. At life. "You gimme this leg, God, now see what you done done! It ain't fair!"

Robert Earner left confused and bewildered with Maddy's words. He understood, but he didn't understand, "We have done nothing." He left off "yet." Because somewhere in his mind, he knew. Of their guilt they were innocent; yet, even in their innocence they knew their guilt. He returned his full mind to his education; he had been steadily saving, planning. With a scholarship and his savings he was on his way to an African-American college, his dream. He did love Lily Bea, but he nodded his head "goodbye" to her, and disappeared from her life.

Not too long after the firing, Maddy became ill and could not work for a month or two. He had always washed all the dry-cleaning possible in the washing machine in the back of the shop. Then he would steam press them hisself. In time, as his health got better, he would still do the washing: just put the clothes in and press the right buttons. He could not do the pressing, though. It was too hard on his leg and back to stand there, pulling down and pushing up the heavy lid of the press.

He showed Lily how to do the pressing. Pressing was hard on her because you had to lift that heavy press and bring it down, then lift it again. All day. She sweated and ached over that press. He lay in his bed, sick, resting, and miserable, wondering, "Lord, a man don't deserve this kind'a bad treatment from no wife! I been a good man! I don't do no sinnin no more!"

Two more years passed in that way. Maddy was still "sick," Lily Bea wasn't singing as she worked anymore. Hadn't for a long time. She never danced, all of a sudden, anymore either. She didn't go to school for any classes anymore. Didn't even think of it.

She was a drudge, and looked it. Her hair stayed wet from the steam so she just kept it wrapped in a rag. The steam didn't hurt or help her skin, but she kept her usual good care of it. We were still friends so we still talked. I told her to always use cold water on her face, to keep her pores from gettin ruined. Her nails were chipped and broken. Who cared? She didn't. She was tired, tired, tired, all the time. She was such a run-down drudging slave, she had given up on life.

One day Sorty came by, smiling, to pick up a "little change." In semiprivate, Maddy told Sorty, "You got to find you a new place to get you some money! We can't trade on this lazy-ass daughter of yours no more." He had taken to swearing at her. "Maybe she helps me a little in the shop, but she don't do nothin in the bed! I got to take care of her, and you ain't helpin me none by comin by here to 'borrow' no money that you don't never tend to pay me back no way!"

Sorty got close to Lily before she left the shop that day. Told her, "What's wrong with you, girl? Don't you see what you got here?! You betta grow up, and get some sense! If you don't, somebody gonna take all this right out from under your nose!"

For the first time, Lily talked back to her mother, "Who? You? Hell, take it, take him! Take the whole damn place, Mama. This what you wanted for me? Well, now this is what I want for you. Take it!" She turned back to the steam press. She slammed the steam press down; it billowed angrily, blowing steam into Sorty's face.

Sorty just looked off into space a quick minute, took a deep breath with no steam in it, slurred her eyes at Maddy, and sauntered on out of the shop. "I was livin fore I knew either one of ya!" The door had almost closed behind her when she stuck her head back in, saying, "I'll be back next week, my rent is gonna be due." She smiled Maddy a "good-bye."

Maddy always took care of all things outside the shop, except for shopping for food. Lily always cooked, so she always had to shop. "The kitchen is a wife's domain!" Maddy said.

Because Lily never did much outside of the shop, Maddy told her, "You don't need to go spendin good money for clothes you don't wear noway." Lily couldn't even afford clothes from the secondhand shops. Again, Maddy told her, "Wear some of these clothes we have done cleaned and ain't never got paid for. Them people ain't never comin back to get em. I ought'a have a sale on em. You pick some of them, fore I sell em."

The only time Lily Bea got money to spend was when she had to shop for food. It was also the only time she had choices she could make for herself; what she wanted to cook. She really relished the few days a month she had to shop for food. It was a time when she would be alone.

Lily Bea would slowly walk by all the little shops with their windows full of food and sundry things. Thinking. "My marriage to a 'businessman' was supposed to make my life better. Now, I'm working harder than I ever have in my life. And . . . it may never end. I still have nothing I can call my own. Not even that damn steam press. I make the money, but he parcels it out to me like I am a child. And I never get to buy anything I really want."

In the markets, her heart beat faster as she looked at all the choices. Not because she could buy all she wanted, but because the limit of the money was the limit of choice. She could buy only one of this or one of that, and not the ones she wanted. She would see all the different things that she would love to eat, her mouth would water, but she could not afford them. She could cut corners and save coupons, but the cutting in no way allowed her to purchase much, or anything exciting, from all the choices in the stores.

Sometimes she just went into a store because the window was so full of appetizing things to drink and eat. She wandered around, looking at the different succulent meats, the breads, the preserves and jams, the wines and champagnes she had read of, but never tasted. In fact, she had never tasted most all of these things.

When she lived with her family it was always "soul food"; now in her own home, Maddy wanted soul food all the time.

Meat and potatos and grease. The small sum of money she had to spend did not allow real choices. She would sigh, "I would really like a lamb chop, with mint jelly, a salad, and a glass of wine with my dinner, just once." For the few moments, with a little money in her hand, she could allow herself to dream.

And dream she did. Lily Bea had always been quiet, alone in her world. So now, with any conversation between Maddy and Lily down to bare necessities, she lived in her mind and books. In dreams. He would often watch her for long periods, surreptitiously, longing for her body. Any body, but Lily especially because her body was supposed to belong to him. When saliva had gathered in the hollows of his mouth, he would swallow and ask her, "What you thinkin bout, woman?"

She would turn her head, almost, to him and answer, "Nothing." If the answer changed, it was, "Bout this work."

During these times he received a special order of delicate silks and laces sent from Mr. Forest, owner of the rich folks' cleaners, the Epitome Cleaners. His first thought was Lily knew how to do that, so he handed them to her, thinking, "She so smart, she done been to school so much! So do the work then!" All he had left to do were the deliveries.

As it turned out, when Lily had completed the work, Maddy really was ill. He could not make the delivery. In the past, because he thought Lily was ugly, he had not wanted her to go out among his better customers. He did not want them to see how his wife looked. "And in them worn out clothes, too," he said to himself.

To Lily he said, "Wear your best clothes. You got to go all way crosstown. When you get there, ask for Mr. Forest. I always talk to the owners, if they there, cause I am a owner. If he ain't there just give it to whoever at the counter. They will give you a check; take it and come directly back here with it. Don't say nothin to him and don't say nothin to anyone else."

She always obeyed. Not from fear. Just, what else could she do? Her spirit was so worn down, so tired, she didn't even care about being ugly anymore. "Anyway, people don't seem to see me, and they don't even stare at me at all, anymore. Besides, so what if people do stare at me?"

In fact, I had noticed that despite Lily Bea's dissatisfaction with sex, almost an abhorrence of it, her body, her skin, exuded a faint misty aura of sexuality to men. Women could see it, too. I did. It seemed like you could almost touch it. It might have come from the fact that her body wanted to be loved. I know she liked Robert Earner, but they never got near that far along in their unexpected feelings. Didn't have a chance, I guess. But, sometimes if you can't let a thing out, it will come out on its own. The sexual aura was there. Maybe that was why some people stared. She never looked ugly to me as she became grown.

The Epitome Cleaners was way across town in the best shopping section of the city. She could walk and save the carfare, or she could take the public transportation and just sit, resting. Her heart lightened at the thought. "And I can look out the windows at the shops and people in the free world. I can even stop at the library, and steal an hour or so for myself."

Lily Bea had decided, with Maddy's approval, to wear gray woolen pants, a fresh, lightly starched white blouse, and a fresh white band around her hair. She was so pleased to be out in the fresh air with no steam in her face, and the sun shining through a light misty rain. Devil whipping his wife, they used to say where I came from.

She sat on the slowly moving bus holding tightly to the box filled with the delicate garments she was to deliver. Bright shops along the street had her full attention. Windows were full of colorful, inviting items: clothes, lamps, food, shoes, hats, and such. Her eyes were filled and spilling over with her thoughts of owning any things so beautiful.

The Epitome Cleaners establishment was, if you can imagine it, a grand place of business. They served the best people, the rich. They handled the uniforms of the best places, their sheets, satin bedspreads and drapes, napkins and linens of the best hotels and restaurants. As well as the gorgeous clothing of the rich. The shop was not extravagantly outfitted, not gaudy. It was simple, but everything was of the best: fine drapes at their wide windows, the polished, shining counters were of mahogany, the shelves were of cedar. You could see on a rack billowing skirts, ruffled somethings half covered with plastic covers, and all like that. Oh, you knew you were around money.

When Lily Bea reached her stop, she was amazed at the

rich array of shops. She slowly made her way to and entered the Epitome Cleaners, her mind in awe at a place grander than any home or place she had ever seen. An ocean stood between her knowledge of the rich, and her own poor life.

She stepped, hesitantly, to the counter where two older men were talking together. One of the well-dressed men was the owner, Mr. Weldon Forest; the other was an old customer and friend of the owner. Lily stood there silently, waiting to be shown what to do next.

The counterperson was, momentarily, in the back of the store. So the owner, Mr. Forest, turned to her and asked, "Yes? May I help you?"

Lily looked at the slightly grey-haired man, in the steel gray suit, and said, "I have brought your . . . order?"

He turned his full attention to her. "What order? For what?"

She answered, and the sound of her voice entered his brain. He was a very sensitive man, a lover of classical music. The voice that was soft, smooth, silken, low, and dreamy enchanted him. He looked her over, without seeming to; she looked nothing like her voice sounded.

Weldon Forest was a tall, fifty-three-year-old, wealthy, married, bored, and lonely man. He loved his wife of thirty-three years, but there was no surprise, no excitement, there. The son he adored had his own business on the East Coast. For years now, his pleasures in life were art, music, and his business. He liked the touch and feel of certain materials. He loved beauty.

Mr. Forest decided to transact his own business with her . . . so to hear more of the sound coming from her lips. The lips through which the beautiful sound had come, in his eyes, were beautiful. He forgot the friend he had been talking to, giving all of his attention to Lily Bea. He prolonged his questions.

"Who are you delivering for?"

"Maddy Nettles. We do your delicates."

"Oh, then you are his helper?"

Lily Bea hadn't known how ashamed she was of Maddy; she looked down at the box still in her arms. "Well, yes sir. I did these things."

"Where do you live? Is this your home, this city?"

"I was born here. I live . . . here."

He wanted to hear more of the voice. He smiled down at her; she continued to keep her eyes down. "I was born here in this city, also. Where did you go to school?"

She looked up, smiling one of her small, hesitant, charming smiles. Her white teeth flashed slightly, quickly. She answered him. With the white teeth showing against the dark skin, he noticed her color. He could think of no other questions to ask her. He realized he was staring at her; he remembered his friend looking at him. He remembered the box she was holding. He reached to take the box from her. "That box must be heavy, give it to me." Her hands were quite warm as he touched them.

It was not his usual job, but he wanted to hear more of her voice, and see her smile again, her eyes. He opened the box and commented on the work she had brought. "Maddy just keeps improving his work. This is very beautifully done. These items look as though they have never been worn."

Lily Bea's heart smiled in pleasure at a compliment for her. She smiled her big smile that so few people ever saw. But Weldon Forest saw the smile that changed her whole face. He thought, "Why, she is a beautiful woman."

Lily Bea looked up in pride. "I did these, sir."

"You . . . you did this work?"

"Yes sir, I love to work with such beautiful things. I just . . ." Suddenly she felt foolish. "I just love to feel them."

His skin began to feel very warm. He could even feel the red blush on his face as he thought, "What is wrong with me?" He said, "Let me see your hands?"

Now she knew why Maddy made her cream her hands and wear gloves when she worked the steam press. She showed Weldon her hands, her long, slender, fine hands with the nails clean and clipped to her flesh. So smooth with the special creams her husband bought for this work at the cleaners. Because you must have nothing that can snag or pull on satins and silks. Brocades were stronger, but silks reacted quickly to everything.

Mr. Forest did not touch strangers easily, but he reached out to take and examine her hands. She smiled up at him, anticipating his approval. He looked into her eyes unexpectantly, and instantly a tiny tingle in his spine made him let her hands go quickly, as he thought, "What is going on here?"

He said to her, with a tremulous smile of his own, "Well, and it is very good work. I hope you shall continue."

Lily's smile faded slowly, even as her heart held to its thrill of being complimented, and she turned to leave. The counterperson had returned.

"Ohhh, wait," Weldon Forest said, "I must pay you, and you must not leave your container. We don't have a check ready, so I will pay you in cash. You can sign for it."

Lily turned back, smile gone, head bent down again. The container was being emptied, she waited to pick it up, and held her hand out for the money. Mr. Forest was not a foolish man; he would not flirt with a strange woman. He was unable to understand, himself, what was happening to him; he thought it nothing.

He watched her write her name as she signed a receipt. He was also unable to help himself when he took the money from the clerk, and reached to hand it to Lily. He took her hand in his, held it as he placed the money in it. She was still looking down at the floor as her hand closed around the money. She turned to walk away.

She was almost at the door, still bemused by the bright richness of the shop, when she heard Weldon ask, "Aren't you going to count it?"

She turned her face to him, and asked, "Do I need to?"

The man was further enchanted by her trust. And, yes, the beauty he saw. He answered, "No, my dear, no, you don't. Not when I pay you. But it makes good business to always count your money." He thought a moment. "And our boy will deliver the next order to you, soon. I'm sure we have some things waiting already."

When she was gone, his friend, who had been patiently waiting and watching, asked, "What was that all about? She was an unattractive Black woman, though she was clean. Do you always give your servers such concern?"

Weldon had regained his sense and composure. "Well, I've been doing business with him a long time." He said, without looking at his friend, "I thought she was rather attractive, but, well . . . you're right." Yet, when he thought of her a moment later, he remembered her beauty. And so it passed. He still wondered what had happened to him. Was something the matter with him?

On her walk home, Lily Bea was not thinking so much of him as she was of his shop. Why should she? She thought she was ugly, and was only embarrassed at her nerve to even talk to him. "But, he was a nice man." She sighed. "I like going to that beautiful store to make the delivery." By the time she reached the library, she could not remember a better day in her life. "Being free is everything. That's what I want to be. Free!" She made a few free dancing twirls as she entered her favorite building.

When she reached her home, Maddy counted the money, saying, "I didn't know he was gonna pay cash. Did you spend any 'a this money, Lily? Cause I need all the money we got comin round here! I'm gonna have to cut your mama down some, I can't afford to keep her and you too! You done been to that library again! I told you we ain't got time for all that readin you want'a do!"

Lily Bea didn't answer. She went to her "room" and lay on the pallet. She smiled at the books she had gotten from the library, and opened one to read. When he hollered to her, she answered, "I'm tired. I'm goin to rest till it's dinnertime, then I'll cook. But, now, I'm going to read."

In a few weeks, when the next bundle of items was received and completed, she delivered them. The owner, Mr. Forest, had specified what date they should be returned because he wanted to be sure he was in the shop when she came.

Time had dulled his memory, but he still remembered the last words his friend had said when Lily Bea had come. He, himself, remembered Lily as being unattractive, "but . . . there was something else about her. I can't put my finger on it." He didn't know why, really, he hadn't forgotten the thing. It wouldn't come clear in his mind. "Was it her voice?" Then, "What am I thinking about? She works for me, for God's sake!"

His boredom and his loneliness made any excitement important to him. Some sense in him remembered the thrill Lily Bea's voice, smile, and touch had given him. He would shake his head in annoyance. "It is absurd that I would even think I had such feelings for a little black woman. A poor working woman, at that."

He had, in the past, had a mistress or two, but it seemed to have added up to lust, not for him, but for his financial help. He was a generous man. But, as to love, he had never "loved" anyone except the woman he had married long ago. "But, these stirrings . . . Just old age, I suppose.

"Maybe I need to take a trip somewhere. But, where? It's all the same every place, no matter where." After a moment's pause, "I could always go back and spend a week looking around the Louvre again. I never see all of it." He brightened a moment, then his dark mood returned. "But Wilhamena won't want to go with me, and I don't want to go alone again." He shook his head, casting the thoughts out of his mind. "I must learn to be satisfied with what life has given me. Who could wish for more?"

The next order from Epitome Cleaners had been sent to the Clean Cleaners, and been completed by Lily Bea. It seems impossible, but she took even more care with the fragile things. "Now that they know it is my work, I want it to be perfect." She also wanted another lovely free afternoon to herself.

Knowing Maddy, as she did, she did not act excited in any way about making the delivery. If he knew she wanted to, he would rub that leg down and make delivery hisself.

For the first time, Mr. Forest had specified when they must be returned. He didn't want to be at the shop all day, so the date and the afternoon were specified. He remembered Lily's face, vaguely, as unattractive, but he remembered her. There was something he could not put his finger on, exactly. He only knew he wanted to be there when, and if, she came.

Maddy's leg, back, and feet really did ache, hurt, and discomfort him. Lily was acting like she didn't want to go, but he would have had to ask her to go anyway.

Lily Bea took a book to read on the bus. She had started smiling in pleasure even a block away from Maddy; she loved the freedom, but she loved the ride across town just as much. The chance to see the better side of the city, the beautiful clothes, the grand homes that the bus passed. Her own dreams, fragilely thin as they were, fluttered, lifted. "Oh, not for me; never for me. But just to know all this beauty, this kind of life, is out here ... for somebody."

A shadow flickered across Lily's face. "It is almost painful to have to travel back to that dim, dark, little, dingy, stingy, strange shop where my life waits for me." She threw those thoughts from her mind so they would not ruin her day. "I have enough of that when I am there!" She opened the book of *World's Art Treasures* she had brought.

Mr. Forest was standing at his wide windows, his arms crossed behind him and a frown on his face as he looked up the street toward the bus stop. He did not have to wait there long. He recognized her by the box she carried. He nodded in her direction, and wondered why he had been thinking of this woman. "She is not attractive, after all. My friend was right."

Lily smiled, in more pleasure, at the man, and the shop, where she had enjoyed herself briefly. He saw that smile, and was transported again. He felt her presence again. He took the box from her, and setting it on the counter, turned back to her, saying, "And, so, you are back. How are you?"

Lily Bea stood there smiling. She even giggled a little, embarrassed or self-conscious, thinking, "He doesn't want an answer."

At her smile, her eyes, her little laughter, he was becoming entranced again. "You must wait to be paid." He reached for her book. "What is that book you have?" She gave the book to him, with the same smile.

"Ahhhhh, art! You are interested in art?"

Lily Bea nodded, and began to speak about the book. She pointed to her bookmark. "I'm reading about Colombian art, but I think I love all art. I'm going to get a book on cathedrals, the ancient cathedrals and temples. I like to study old and strange architecture and art. But they had some special pieces in this book, so I took it out."

Her voice, passed from her lips like misty, cultured pearls, went through his ears, encircling his brain, gently, marvelously. The sound quieted his nerves. They spoke, over the book, at length. Her voice hypnotized him. "She is beautiful," he thought.

Weldon Forest wanted to give her something. (His heart was a generous one.) As he listened to her, he looked at her manner, her clothes. He thought, "Surely, a little Negro lady would like a lot of things. And this lady likes books, as well."

He felt her powers, her gifts, though he did not understand his feelings. But, the next time he had things for the Clean Cleaners, he took them down his own self.

You may know there is a quality, a gift, some people have. It emanates from their heart and spirit. It imbues their body with an aura that issues from their mind, through their skin . . . to other people who have receptive hearts and minds: those who have beauty in their souls. Lily Bea's mind was more innocent than some children. It was such a glowing gift. Ephemeral beauty . . . unseen, but felt, in certain people. By the right eyes, hands, and hearts. It must be God Who gives this gift. It is given to few, yet . . . Mystical. Magical. All the taunting, all the pain, in Lily Bea's childhood caused part of her to huddle, far back, into someplace that was serene and beautiful. She's still at home there; but her beauty comes out to you, if you have beauty in you.

Weldon Forest drove himself to take the next delivery, early, to the Clean Cleaners and Lily Bea. He saw Maddy, with the angry crippled leg propped up on a table, jump up on his crippled leg and grin, saying, "Ohhh, Mr. Forest, bossman! How come you to come down here? I coulda come and got those things! Or my wife, Lily here, woulda been glad to pick em up!"

Weldon Forest's heart flinched and fell when he heard the word *wife*. He looked at Lily, who looked miserably embarrassed. Weldon saw none of the beauty. Her face was long and sad. Her eyes were of sorrow. She attempted to smile at Mr. Forest, but lost the effort because there was no light around him. It was vanquished by the dimness of her husband's shop.

Mr. Forest looked at Maddy, saying, "Your wife? I didn't know you had a wife."

Maddy was ashamed to have someone ugly to be his wife. He laughed, a stingy, dirty little laugh, said, "Well, sometimes you take what you can get, Mr. Forest. She a good girl, though."

Mr. Forest left, thinking, "A girl? Take what you can get? I was out of my mind." But there lingered in his mind those little thrills, that voice. Then he remembered, Lily had said nothing. Hadn't even smiled. He didn't go back to his shop or to his house. He drove to some favorite place of his that was filled with mountains, trees, birds, sky, and clouds. He sat there a long time. His eyes filled with tears that never fell; they just dried, evaporated. Then he drove back to his life. "I don't know what I was expecting."

Lily Bea would not do any delivery again. Her life just continued as usual for the next three months or so. She started taking some of the money they took in, for herself. She took to getting her hair done. She kept it up, even when Maddy said, "We ain't got no money to waste on your head!"

They did have money. She knew where it was hidden away. She began to take that bus ride, get off at a good place, and go in to buy things for herself. Little things, not too expensive. And she put some away for herself.

In her daily movements she noticed the pharmacist, the counterman, the meat-market man, just different men she had to talk to. She noticed they wanted to talk more, be nicer, liked to touch her. She didn't seek these attentions, they just were. She began to feel a power, her power as a woman, however little. Lily did not understand the power, did not seek to use it. But this knowledge of herself cracked the door open to a freedom to like herself. To even love herself. To let herself be seen . . . a little more. Not by anyone in particular, just anyone.

Lily Bea, in her private, quiet moments, thought of Weldon Forest. "He is older, but he is very nice. Kind. The world looked different when I was around him. It looked . . . happy. I really like him."

Doing her work around the shop, she was still called ugly. Always ugly. I knew that was the loop Maddy was hanging her with.

I said little things to make her know that herself. As usual, she did not hate, or even despise, anything but her own (she thought) crooked body, and her husband who still grabbed her body in the nights, greedily, whenever he could. Often, he tried to sneak on top of her when she was on her pallet, asleep. She always woke up, screaming.

Lily Bea wanted to leave Maddy, was saving money to that end. But where to go? No place she knew, and she still didn't have much money even if she did know. My house was full of grandchildren; I offered her my space, but she wanted her own space.

Now, life is strange, you know that already.

Lily Bea was on Weldon Forest's mind. More than he thought was natural. But, he was still a man who felt few thrills or interests. His was a good wife, though she had long taken him, and life, for granted. She thought they would both always be there. He seemed invisible at home, until she gave a dinner or gathering. His son always wanted his dad to visit him in the East. But he didn't want to pack a suitcase just for three or four days, and he couldn't enjoy staying any longer.

So . . . he thought of Lily Bea. More than liking her so much; she could talk about interesting things, and she was a puzzle to him. When he thought of her, he felt just the slightest thrill-twinge in his mind and heart. Thoughts that gave him any kind of thrill or just reminded him of any thrill, were often on his mind.

Weldon divined that Lily Bea must be terribly unhappy in the old cleaning shop. There had not been a bit of happiness in her face, or even a hint of the beauty he had seen there in the past.

One morning Weldon decided, "I have to do something." He called the Clean Cleaners and asked that Lily Bea be sent to pick up an order because he had a few questions to ask her about a new fabric.

Maddy had answered the phone. He said, "Oh, don't worry bout her, Mr. Forest. I can take care of that all right. I'll be right on over there to see bout things."

Mr. Forest's mind formed a plan without his permission or thought. He told Maddy, "Well, all right. But I am going to send a package of books to your place. I want you to give them to your . . . Lily Bea. They are about fabrics. I want her to read them. Then I want to talk to her about some new fabrics, and systems. Do you understand, Maddy? She has studied these things; she will know what I mean."

"Oh, yes, sir."

"Maddy, does Lily still do all my work orders?"

"Yes, sir. I have taught her and she knows. I watch and see what she does. When they leave here, I know they right."

"I'm sure you do. Still, I want Lily to come to my office so I can discuss some things with her. She can tell you when she returns . . . home."

"Yes, sir. Sure will. Thank you, sir." They hung up. Maddy grinned, proud of his business-self. Weldon to sit back in his plush grey leather chair, thinking. Under his breath, he said to God, "I never lied once."

The order with two books was sent that day: one book on new European fabrics from France and Italy and their care; another on cathedrals, thick with pictures from France, Italy, and England.

Maddy called out to Lily where she was cleaning their house. "He done sent a order of work for you and a coupl'a books for you to read. You betta read them things. We in business to make money, and he the money-man. I'll cook my own dinner or just heat somethin up."

Lily Bea was drudging in the rooms behind the cleaning shop in the kitchen, which had no light of joy in it. She heard Maddy's words and could hardly wait to see the books, but she didn't want to appear excited to her husband. She moved into Maddy's bedroom, hastily smoothed the covers, and turned quickly away from his bed. Maddy cared nothing for symmetry, or harmony of the furniture in the rooms. The "furniture" was mismatched pieces from secondhand stores or the dump.

When they married he had said, "This all we need." He laughed as if it was a pleasant joke. "These things, and us, all look the same in here in the dark: broken and used." He always included her because he needed her ugliness to make her as crippled as he was. He never complimented her, not even on her special work. He would look over the fine work she had done and tell her, "Oh, it's all right." There was no joy in her life. And lately, it had reached the place where she did not know how she could continue living her life.

Her heart grieved so much from her life, recently she had gone to her mother, Sorty. Sorty had listened, with another glass of gin in her hands, bought with the money Maddy gave her every month. Said something like, "Chile, you lucky! We all got a cross to carry, but, at least, your belly is full, and you got a man to help you carry your burden. You betta count your blessins! I wish a good man would come take care me!

"You got to r'member, Lily Bea, you ain't no pretty woman! I'm your mama, and I'm gon to tell you the Lord's truth. You a ugly woman and you lucky you got any man at all!" Sorty believed these words. Both of them did.

The morning the order arrived with the books Lily Bea had been thinking of all these things as she cleaned. "I'm so glad I don't have a child from this man." She tried to picture a life of love and happiness, but her mind couldn't make the picture come alive for her. "Soon I will be old, and . . . something . . . there must be more to life than this. Life will have passed me by. Just an ugly, nobody wants, woman in this world."

The tears were rolling down her cheeks when Maddy called out to her about the package.

Holding back her eagerness to run to the books, she began dusting a half-blackened mirror and, looking up, she saw herself: ugly. She sighed, saying, as she moved away, "Lord, I'd rather be alone. But how? Where? I don't have more than a hundred dollars hidden away. And I'm not going back to my mama's." She began to silently cry from her heart. Her body and her heart were so lonely. So hungry and so lonely.

She felt so disheartened her body started moving to the waves of her sorrow. A slow, swaying, dirge. Her body moved smoothly, even in the cramped space. Her eyes closed. She was thinking to herself, "My life and I are one big zero. Every day." She prayed, "Deliver me, please God. Deliver me."

Maddy was jealous of Mr. Forest's request for Lily Bea, but he respected him too much to try to deny the request. "Besides," Maddy thought, "I am getting older, my leg givin me more trouble lately. I'ma have to let her do more round here. Let her take care me for a while! Let her see how she like that! I have a wife don't like no lovin! So, work fool!" (He had never explained to anyone how his leg came to be crippled. He was not born with it that way. It was an angry leg and his whole face was angry with the movement of that leg. He was pitiful in his own right. But, one wondered, if he did not blame an accident? or someone else? had the fault been his own?)

When Lily Bea came to him, Maddy said, "Mr. Forest sent this order over here to my shop, and he sent a package, a book, for you to read about how to do your work better. So if you finished cleanin and cookin, you can read it. I'll take care the regista."

He gave the books to Lily. "You take these work books and go head. Study and see what he talkin bout. I'll do this order. You forget I taught you most all you know, and I don't need you to do everything I do."

I don't have to tell you, when Lily Bea took the package of books, she felt both pleasure and importance. She made a cup of tea, and went to her pallet to settle down and read. She opened the smallest book first: the fabric systems book. It looked interesting. Then she opened the art book, and was lost for several hours in beauty, history, and dreams. She thanked Weldon Forest from her heart. Maddy didn't pay her any attention because he wasn't interested in books.

The Epitome Cleaners' order was finished in three days; the books had been read, and it was time for Lily Bea to deliver.

When Lily arrived to see Weldon, her hair was done neatly, and she was wearing a secondhand, simple but good, dress. She was smiling and looked nearly happy. Weldon smiled down at her as he shook her hand. He held it awhile as they spoke.

She was carrying a book in her hand she had read on the bus. Maddy hadn't wanted the driver-man to pick her up. "Ain't no sense in botherin that man! You can make it over there on your own!"

Weldon Forest was, unexpectedly, nervous. After he indicated to the counterperson to take the basket, he saw the book Lily took out of it. "What is that book, Lily?"

"Fairy tales, Mr. Forest. And I loved that book you loaned me. I loved it!"

Weldon smiled, delighted. "Fairy tales? For a woman your age? Why do you still like fairy tales?"

"Wishes that come true. Golden apples and carpets that can fly you to some magic land of dreams." She smiled, and he reached out in too great a haste. Self-conscious, he was glad the book was there to sidestep being too forward. He touched her whole hand and the book.

"Let me see it. I have read a few fairy tales in my time." He leafed through the pages, looking at them and her.

When he handed the book back to her, he did not release the

book that she half held in her hand. He felt her presence, greater than ever. She smiled questioningly at him.

He still held her hand as he said, "Lily, I have been thinking. I might open a little specialty shop . . . just to handle silks and delicates. Even sell a few imported things."

Lily pressed his hand in her hand, and let it go. "Oh! that would be nice, Mr. Forest. That will be more work for me."

He placed his hand on her shoulder, leading her to his simple but rich office. "Let us go into my office. I want to talk to you about this." Lily felt fear that something was ending, and excitement that something might be beginning. When they were seated, Weldon leaned toward her, saying, "Well, you see, I had something else in mind, Lily. And call me Weldon, please, and I will keep calling you 'Lily.' We are . . . friends, in a way." Lily smiled, and looked down at the floor.

"Look up, Lily. Look at me, please. Listen, I want you to think about this. I know your . . . husband"—she frowned, and Weldon took note—"owns a cleaning business, but I wondered if you would . . . manage my new specialty shop?"

Suddenly, Weldon looked like a piece of heaven to Lily Bea. With a surprised gasp, a glow slowly covered her face. "Mr. Forest, ahh, Weldon. I would be so happy to have a real job. Make money for myself." She couldn't stop herself. "Have a different life."

Weldon cleared his throat and said, "I know this is personal, Lily"—her glow gave him courage—"but, are you . . . happy, Lily?"

He liked to say her name. "You didn't look happy in your, ah, that shop."

She took a moment before she answered. "I don't know anything about being happy, Weldon. I only know about work. I . . . I have been wanting to leave . . . the shop, but I have nowhere . . ." She stopped, realizing she was telling this man, this almost stranger she barely knew, her secret business. "But, it is the truth," she thought, so she continued. "I would like to be alone, for a change. I have to work, and I want to, but,"—she looked around his office, then closing her eyes, said to him, "I would like some nice things of my own. *My* own. Not just touch them when I clean them. Have a few things of *my very own* . . ."

She opened her eyes. Weldon had leaned back, he was smiling, slightly, nodding his head slowly, and gently rocking in his chair. He lowered his head, his eyes looking directly into hers. He spoke softly but firmly, "Would you mind . . . if I helped to place a few of those things at your disposal? You would owe me nothing. Not one thing. Now or ever." She nodded her head. "Yes." His heart began beating happily, as he reflected, "I can tell myself I am doing a good deed for this young woman, but it is making me happy. I am really doing it for myself."

They discussed more of the matters their new business entailed, making outlines and notes. Mr. Forest had his secretary type them up for clarity, each taking a copy to add to or change. "In a few days, we will talk again. We'll know how these plans are working out, and any changes we should make."

He wanted to shake her hand, but decided he did not want to frighten her. He leaned forward again, saying, "Well, that settles it. I have been looking at a few places, just tentatively, of course. A few places near here. Vacant business rentals are difficult to find. So, when you can, you might look them over, see what you think?" Lily was smiling, or grinning, and nodding yes to everything he said.

Her eyes widened at his next words. "I will give you a quarter interest in the new shop. And . . . as time passes, you can purchase more. As much as a half interest in the shop, and be working for yourself. You will be the mistress. The shop will belong to me and you. I will have the contract drawn up by my lawyer . . . no one will be able to take it from you. You can have your own lawyer approve it." They both smiled at that. She had no lawyer. So he added, "Get a lawyer. Learn to take care of your business."

Then, he was blessed with such a rare smile, full of gratitude, wonder, disbelief, and joy. She said, "I would also like to go back to school. I want to know . . . everything I can. I will pay my own way." She had never been so beautiful to him.

"Whatever you like, Lily. That is a business expense. It will be deducted from the business."

He wanted to touch her. He knew it was too soon. She would never understand it because he didn't. Instead, he said, "Shall we shake on it?" He took her hand, holding it tightly, and felt that thrilling pleasure in his spine that spread through his shoulders. He held her hand between both of his for the longest time possible.

Lily was thinking, "Golden apples, flying carpets, and Mr. Forest."

In a moment, Weldon said, "Now, we must decide how . . . you want to do this. Do you want to tell Maddy Nettles now?"

Lily Bea shook her head, saying, "No, not now. How long do you think it will take to have the shop opened?"

"At least two months. You can start working before then, however, because there is so much to do. I have a list I've been keeping of three places for you to see. To see which might be the best place."

"I don't know things like that, Mr. Weldon."

Weldon smiled, he had so much time on his hands, full of nothing. "Then I will show you. And we need to plan a grand opening." He was so glad to have a new kind of life, an interest again. A new friend . . . he really liked. "Soon, you will need a place to stay near the business. I don't see how you can live with Maddy while the new shop is being readied."

Lilly Bea started to say, "My mother—"

But Weldon interrupted her, "A small place, one you can be comfortable in until you want to make a change. I will lend you six months' rent, and you can pay me when you are able. Which won't take long once the shop is opened. At the grand opening, the very best people will know we are there to serve them in our new focus and capacity." Lily could only stare at him with wide, round eyes. "And you will need a car. Do you drive?"

Weldon Forest had introduced her to his employees as the manager of a new department. He was leading her to the entrance door as he offered to drive her home, or let the shop-driver take her. She chose to take the bus. "I want to be alone awhile. I'll walk and take a bus." Like a flying carpet, she walked on clouds, and thought and thought and thought. "I don't know why, God, but thank You for this blessing. Please help me do it right. You are delivering me. I will earn it. I will! I will!"

Weldon Forest was very pleased. He wanted to keep this new thrill of his life, the happiness of being alive. And the little Black woman gave this to him. He could not understand why some people thought she was unattractive. "She is so beautiful to me!"

Maddy had long been agitated at all the attention Lily was getting. He wondered if someone would care for, or lie to, Lily Bea enough to try to make sex with her. "It's certain it's not that wealthy, bigshot, Mr. Forest! He in a whole nother world different from us!"

While she had been listening to Weldon Forest that day, changing her life, Maddy had been rifling through her personal things, her drawers, her books, everywhere and everything she touched. Looking for some clue to her small, new independence. There was an air about her of stretching out, breathing deeper; her eyes were bright, even when she wasn't smiling. Maddy tightened his lips as he thought, "It's somethin goin on round here, and I betta find out, cause I pay the bills round here. I'm the man in this house!"

But when she reached home, he didn't bother her. Just

watched her, waiting to be noticed, and feared, himself. She smiled, said hello, and went straight to her pallet with her books.

It was later, when she served his dinner plate, waving a slice of bread in his hand as he chewed his food, he spoke to her. "Don't you be no fool, Lily. Don't let some lying man tell you no lies and mess up your life. I give you a home when you didn't have none but your mama's! And you didn't even have that!" She answered him with silence.

So he continued. "What you doin all this bathin and dressin and goin out this shop all the time for?" He got up to go to the sink to refill his water glass. He limped on his angry leg toward her. "You ain't makin love with me no more. What you doin when you go out? This shop needs regular time, and I need regular lovin. I tole you that when I married you!" She gently shook her head, remaining silent.

Lily was not there when he spoke to Sorty when she came in for "her" money. He told her, "I don't know what done got into your daughta, but you betta talk to her! She ain't treatin me right! I b'lieve she is breakin her weddin vows . . . cause, I use to get a lit-tle lovin, now and then. Now, she ain't givin me no lovin at all! That ain't right! And you know it! Now . . . I can't keep givin you money every time you ask for it, if I don't get nothin when I ask for it!"

Sorty left empty-handed, shaking her head, thinking, "What is that little ugly-ass Lily Bea doing? I don't care what she do with Maddy, but she messin with me, now! I need my money!"

First chance she got, she said to Lily, "Lily Bea! You ain't bein no fool and doin nothin that would make Maddy quit you and throw you back home on me, are you?! Cause there ain't no room here for another grown woman! You betta think about what you got! Security! And a place of business, and a home. That ole cripple ain't gonna live too much longer, then it all be yours!"

Lily thought to herself, "Once a person has a dream almost coming true, and a future that looks brighter than any star I have ever seen, that ole security is not enough to stop my dream. It may not be an apple made of gold, and it don't have to be. But my dream is getting more golden every day."

The days passed along slowly, but, at last, the day did come for Lily Bea to leave. Weldon had thought it best to start a divorce for her, so the business would be "hers." The papers were ready to be served. Her new, small, but very nice apartment was clean and airy, with a view of a lake. She danced around that apartment each time she carried a few of her belongings and books there. She had so little to take with her, her husband had not noticed anything was gone.

Maddy had been carrying his anger around daily. It showed in his body language, as they say. It was in his eyes and certainly in his voice. He had talked down to her so long, he couldn't find a way to put any softness or tenderness in his voice. He was, also, realizing he loved her, "or somethin."

He hadn't really believed she would leave him, at first. He couldn't know anything for certain, but he was having such strong feelings about her leaving him. He thought she was just being used and lied to. "Who would want her enough to do somethin like give her a position? she keep lyin about? and take her away from her husband? Her own business? Where was her brain? Don't she know she have somethin here? Security? And a future? Nobody else was gonna love her; she was ugly."

Maddy wasn't too sure about her ugliness anymore. Now that she was never there, she had begun to look better to him. He sighed, thinking, "Now, I'm the husband! And I'm gonna have to pay somebody to help me round here, while she help somebody else. Somethin ain't right!" He was hating her, but he was loving her at the same time.

He had told her, "You know if you take that position, and it's a fool thing to do, cause you got your own position here. You own it. You the boss here. I ain't that hard to get along with. And . . . we both got . . . things that don't look good to other people. But we still got each other. If you let me make more love to you, you wouldn't be actin like this. I know what's wrong wit'cha! You need some lovin, girl!"

Lily kept, always, her voice low, soft. The Bible said a soft word turns away wrath. She tried to remain silent, to never say anything at all. She would smile gently at Maddy. Smiling was easier to do, now that she was leaving him. She could not find hate in her heart anyway, it was too happy. She just, quietly, kept moving into her new life.

On her last day, she looked around the ole Clean Cleaners, her "home" for more than seven years. She talked to herself before she talked to Maddy. "Today, today is my last day, my last hours, here where my life has lived and died, for my mama. Now, I'm alive again. No more dim, empty, pitiful life with a pitiful man in this dim, pitiful shop with the washing machine in back. Cheating people." She sighed at life. "Oh, God, I don't want to be sinful or wicked. I don't want to be a sinner, but must I suffer here, in this place, to live right? I didn't want this ... marriage. I never loved Maddy. You said honor your mother; and I did what she said. Now, I want to honor myself, and always honor You. I don't think you mean misery for me, or anyone. I can't stay here. I must go," she sighed, "into some light, some air. Fragrant light air, and days. I'll work hard. I'll go to church more. I love You. I'm afraid to thank You; You might not have sent Weldon. But, I pray You are in this with me. I don't want to live against You. I love You. I am being driven through my life by my life itself."

When she sat down with Maddy, she told him, "Sometimes a chance comes along in life to realize your dreams. I have to go, Maddy."

Maddy looked stupefied. "It ain't nothin but a job. Is that your dream? You got a dream right here then. You own your job here, Lily."

Lily Bea shook her head, gently. "It's not the same thing, Maddy."

He almost snarled, "You takin my work for that man from me!"

"I'm taking nothing, Maddy. I'm leaving everything here."

"You leavin everything here? I paid for everything you got, Lily!"

Her voice was less soft. "I worked here too. I'm leaving everything but my books and a few personal, small things."

"I knew you didn't love me! You a bitch! You never did love me!"

After a moment's silence, Lily said, "I believe I loved you as much as you loved me."

"You a lyin bitch, bitch!"

She tilted her head, saying, "Do you really think you are worth lying to?"

He stood up over her. "Are you gettin a divorce, too?!"

Slowly, Lily stood up also. She thought, "I don't want to lie, but I can't tell him now. He is angry and we are alone. I must stay calm and smooth." She listened to the sound of every word he said; she watched, and felt, every breath he took. At last, she said, "I'm not thinking of a divorce." Which was almost true, she was thinking of his anger. And leaving.

She moved away from him, toward the door, as she put on her little rabbit-fur coat, then she turned around, came back, and, for the first time, she hugged him. "Good-bye."

When the door closed behind her, Maddy sat down and stared at the last place she had been standing. He started rocking in his chair; it was not a rocking chair. He rocked and rocked. Then he cried. Hard, little, broken sobs, from a hard, little, broken man.

Lily Bea drove to her mother's house; she parked the car at some distance and walked the rest of the way. Her caution was instinctual; she just didn't feel it was time to let everyone know all her business.

In the recent past, Sorty had lost two of her children: a son to AIDS, a daughter to alcoholism. There was only one daughter besides Lily Bea left, the pretty one, Reella. Reella had four children, and was on her way to alcoholism.

Now, here was Lily Bea telling her she was going to leave Maddy. Sorty looked at Lily a long moment, took a long drink, put her glass down, and said, "What's going on in your head? You done read all the books, and lost your mind. You leavin a good man, with a good business?"

Sorty looked up to heaven, saying, "Lord, I done give birth to a pure-dee fool!" Lily sighed, but said nothing. Looking in her glass, Sorty continued, "All my children's almost gone!" She took a swallow, looked at Lily, and said, "Two children left and one done lost her mind!"

Sadly, Lily looked at her mother, saying, "Their way was clear when they were born; their exit almost came with their entrance into this world."

Sorty looked at her, snapping, "You damn right! You right, but you ain't good-lookin at all, and you the one that have a home and a future with security. And you gettin ready to be a fool! If you was smart, you'ud keep Maddy. He's your last chance! And he ain't gonna help me with my rent no more! What you gonna do bout that!?"

Lily sat on the edge of a chair, saying, "Why don't you go to work for him, Mama? He needs a helper."

Sorty snorted, "You his helper! Lily Bea, you ain't bein no fool and doin nothin that would make Maddy really quit you, and throw you back home, here on me, are you? You are Maddy's true wife! Before God and everybody! You his wife!"

"Well, I have decided to be my own wife, my own everything."

"You a selfish bastard, Lily."

Lily sighed, saying, "You know, Mama, when I was young I had a little flame in me. I wanted to do something with my life, but you took that flame, burned me with it until I burned down to ashes. Now you want me to stay where you put me, for your advantage, until I'm only a little pile of ashes. I'm trying to get that flame back. I don't want to be just ashes." She stood up as she continued, "I want to give you an address; if you drop a note to me, I will call you."

"Call me!? What good that gonna do me? Who gonna help me with some money? Who you goin to work for anyway?"

"That is not important."

Sorty laughed an ugly laugh. "Yes, ma'am, it is! Who gon help me? Is it that white man who pretendin he like you? And lettin you run over other people's lives? He teachin you to be white?"

"It's a job, Mama, that's all."

"Then why can't I know where it's at?"

"There is nothing there for you. I don't want you coming there."

"You shamed of me?"

"No more than you are of me."

Sorty took another swallow. "I never been shamed of you. Are you goin to help me? From your new job?"

"I'll have to see what I need first."

"You put yourself before me? Your mother?"

"Mama, I have learned that seems to be the way things go with you."

Sorty sighed.

Lily turned to go. "I'm going. You'll hear from me, Mama."

"Well, bring me, or send me, some money. And remember, I love you; you my chile. You can always count on me. That's why you know I'm tellin you the truth when I tell you to stay with that good man you got. I didn't have to worry bout my rent; he'll change now."

As Lily Bea went out her mother's door, she said, "You know, Mama, you can have him. I wouldn't mind at all. At least, go to work for him. I don't know when I'll have some way to give you your rent." She looked at her watch. "I have to go now. I'm late."

Sorty, ever alert, asked, "You drivin a car? Whose car?"

Lily started closing the door behind her. "You take care yourself, Mama; I'll take care of myself."

Sorty hollered at her, "You a ungrateful bastard!"

Just before Lily closed the door, she said, "I may be a bastard, Mama." The door shut, Lily was gone.

Sorty upended her glass as she watched Lily walk away. "That bast— that bitch got a car!" Sorty had never had a car. She fixed a fresh drink (she always had money for that), sat down in a worn chair, staring at the door through which her rent, and help, had gone. She didn't rock, she just stared and stared at that space. She was trying to think of a new way. A new way to live.

Maddy was finally served the divorce papers. He stared at them as if they were from Mars. Then he closed the cleaners, and ran to her mother's house. Waving the papers, he told Sorty, "Lily might as well never try to come back to me and my bizness. That's all over now! I don't know what she'd have to do when she come back."

Sorty looked at Maddy hopefully, saying, "Well, she is comin back! Just wait till she find out how cold them people really is, out there in this world! She'll realize what she had here at home! We'll see her behind coming back, yet!"

But Sorty could not really help Maddy. The one time she had seen her since Lily left, Lily never did speak of her plans. She had been quiet, listening to her mother tell her, "Girl, you better come on back home to Maddy! Wake up, and smell the money, honey!"

Lily Bea just lived on in the reality of her new world. She worked hard during the day. Mr. Forest did not really have to be there. She had decided to always call him "Mr. Forest" around his employees. He appreciated her sensibility. But he was there at every reasonable opportunity, smiling, suggesting, helping in some way. He was never not a gentleman.

One thing Weldon noticed was that all the businesspeople they had appointments with, even the deliverymen who came to the new shop, never looked at Lily Bea with any interest at all. Didn't even look into her face long. Over time, though, he noticed as her nervousness went away, as Lily Bea's joy in the business bloomed on her face, they looked long at her smile. They even asked extra, unnecessary questions just to hear her voice.

Mr. Jacob, the jeweler from next door, visited often just to ask her questions. Weldon pondered as he watched the change. They were attracted to her! Just as he was! He began to guard her, tried always to be there if a few special businessmen were due. She did not belong to him, but she was his. This beautiful woman.

He opened accounts for her. "You have to be very well dressed in such a business; it's especially good for our kind of business." She had better sense than to go too far. She did not look too sophisticated, nor too much a counterperson. She looked just right in her simple, classic styles. Smart, plain black shoes with two-inch heels. Lily Bea's brains were almost popping out of her head, it was filled with so much joy. "It's like my own fairy tale."

The flyers about the grand opening had gone out, as well as invitations to some customers. She hadn't wanted to use her name, Lily, in the shop's name. It might lead Maddy and her mama to her. She chose to name it "the Flowers," a "Specialty Cleaning Shop." Besides the cleaning of delicates, it was stocked with items of fragile, lacy female things to purchase, and even some exquisite silk ties for men.

The evening of the opening he took her out to an early dinner. Well, what could be more innocent? Their friendship was still an innocent one. But he was old enough, and wealthy enough, not to care what talk would come from seeing him out with a young Negro lady smiling across a table at him. "We are business partners."

He smiled down at her as he asked, "Wear something nice, Lily. One of your new dresses, with the respectably lowered neckline, the buyer just sent over to you. Please?"

She had laughed, saying, "Of course. I needed help to know what to wear to the opening anyway."

Quite a few older, bored people, and those with business interests, came to the opening. Champagne and finger foods were served by formal waiters. Well, they were serving the "best" people, the richest women in the city, the larger department store owners and their wives. Mr. Jacob, the jeweler, came without his wife. "She had another appointment," he said, chewing on crackers and crab, and staring at Lily Bea.

Lily was dressed smartly, in good business taste. Her funny little body looked very attractive. Her shyness and happiness showed in her face, flowing from her smile. Many of the women saw only ugliness in a nice dress when they looked at her. Many of the gentlemen were much attracted to her. They listened closely, carefully, to every word she said about the shop and its services.

Her charisma flowed from her; the fire of her dreams and charms of her inner beauty quite shone through, spreading out, filling the shop. She was plain, but not drab . . . at all. One gentleman told Weldon, "The lady, your manager, is a *belle laide* in my country."

Weldon watched the men, thinking, "Perhaps I will not be the only one to discover my jewel. I need to make some plan to keep her to myself." It was true.

Some of the men began to bring their wives' satin gowns and silk lingerie to the Flower Cleaners. They let their servants pick the clothing up, but found excuses to stop by to see when the garments would be ready. Not one of them really knew why they were so charmed by Miss Kneed. (She used her maiden name.) A few gentlemen, working below the waist, even ventured to ask Lily out, on hidden, and secret, dates. She always refused because she understood, but she didn't understand, Why?

Within a month or so, Weldon knew he was in love with her. Deeply in love. She was like a narcotic he could never get enough of.

He had arranged for her to move into a larger, two-bedroom apartment. He would come to her shop at closing time, then follow her to her apartment, or meet her there to talk business over a glass of crisp, cool wine while she broiled a steak or a fillet of fish for the both of them. He liked the way she cooked, the way she did everything.

He never touched her familiarly, he was always a gracious gentleman. Their general amiability and kindness brought them close. They both had bashful feelings, and a delicacy of expression, which made it pleasant to be together.

Lily Bea's new life was a million miles away from her old, past life. She could not believe such a dream could be for her, "but it is happening to me, every day." She thanked God, every day, for making her love books, to read, and to love learning. She thought those were the reasons she was where she now was, manager of her own (almost) shop.

Weldon paid her lavish compliments. He came very close, several times in the past year, to telling her he loved her, but was afraid he would lose any opportunity to be near her. There were frustrating times when he thought, "It has to become a closer relationship. I don't want my feelings to remain hidden, a treasure only for me. I want to hold her, I want her body close to mine. I want to be inside her mind and her body." He thought about it almost constantly.

His own business offices saw more of him, during the last year, than they could remember. His private secretary knew, but didn't know all. She had to work with Weldon so she studied him. "Why in the world, when, if he wanted a girlfriend, he could have really pretty women?" Then she would remember her own plain, shoulder-slumped husband, and smile to herself. She was a good secretary; she kept his personal business in her mind.

It had been a little over a year when, one evening over their glass of wine, Weldon spoke to Lily Bea in a certain way. "Lily, dear, I have been thinking about affairs of the heart." She smiled a little, giving him her entire attention. He continued, "What do you think of love? Do you ever think of it, love?"

She thought a moment, in silence, then answered, "Everyone thinks of love, sometime."

"I'm not asking everyone, Lily, I am asking you what *you* think of love."

"Well, Weldon, I think it must be one of the most wonderful things in this world. It's the only thing that makes anything beautiful. Worth having. I also think it is very hard to find, to have. People seem to have such a problem with it, at least the people I have known."

"Have you ever loved anyone, Lily? I mean, I know you were married, once. Did you love him?" He lowered his head, still looking at her, and asked again, "Have you ever been in love?"

"I have . . . good feelings about . . . some people. I have good feelings about you. All your kindness, and the things you have done for me. You might say . . . I love you . . . in a way."

His heart expanded buoyantly in his chest, and he reached his hand across the table toward her as he said, "Do you mean that, Lily? Could you, do you, love me . . . a little?"

She became nervous, thinking, "What is he asking? What does he want?" She laughed gently and slapped his hand lightly. "Who could help but love you? Of course I love you. You are my friend; my best friend. I have no other."

He looked at his empty hand a moment, then started to withdraw it, but left it lying there, waiting. "I want you to love me . . . more than a friend." He took a deep breath. "Because, you see, I am in love with you. More than a friend. I love you."

She did not take his hand, yet. But she continued gently smiling at him. In a very soft voice, she asked, "What could we do with love, Weldon? You are married. You have a life. I have a different life. Even if we love each other, what would, what could, we do?" They sat in silence for several moments. He withdrew his open palm from the table, placing it out of sight in his lap.

Her nervousness tightened her throat. She reached her hand across the table as she said, "Oh, Weldon, you have done so much for me; my life is different, my world is different, everything I know is different. No one could help loving someone who has done all you have done for me. But you will not lose; the shop is doing great, making money. I sell a lot of things. But, I will sign it back over to you; I will not take advantage of your kindness, your thoughtfulness. I know you felt sorry for me, so you gave me a chance, an opportunity. I had hoped I could pay you back, in some way, so you would know . . ."

He flinched at the words *pay you back*. He stood up to leave, as he thought, "This is not what I wanted. If I can never have her love . . . I'm a foolish old man to have wanted so much from her. I'll just leave her alone, as long as she remains somewhere close to me."

He said aloud, "Lily, you are the business. It is your business. I wasn't trying to . . . buy you. We are both making money in our business. You owe me nothing. It has been my pleasure to even have you near enough to talk to. My life was like being alone in a desert . . . having to talk to myself. You have changed my life also."

She was silent as she watched him get ready to leave. She hadn't treated him as a guest for a long time. He knew where his coat and hat were; he had put them wherever they were. He was not a guest, he was really at home, in her mind. A little love bubbled up in her mind, or was it pity? There was no reason to pity him. Love? Gratitude? Lily sighed, and rose to see him out.

He stopped her. "Don't get up. I'll see myself out. And, my dear friend, I'll probably see you tomorrow!" Then he was gone.

Lily Bea didn't see him again for almost two weeks. She left several messages with his secretary, Mrs. Gaines, for him to call her. She asked Mrs. Gaines, "Is he all right? Is he sick? Has anything happened to him?"

All Weldon's employees thought Lily was just another employee in management. Besides, she was African-American. "Nothing wrong with her, just, Mr. Forest surely wouldn't, well, you know. He is strictly business."

Mrs. Gaines could hear the sincere concern in Lily's voice, so she answered, "Sometimes he goes out of town, Miss Kneeds. He runs his business so well, we roll along without him. He'll show up any day now, or I'll hear from him, and let you know. Do you have an emergency, or anything I can do?"

"No, Mrs. Gaines, things are just fine over here, too. I was just a little worried when I . . . You're right; he is probably just fine. He deserves a little time . . . Oh, never mind. Thank you, Mrs. Gaines, and you don't have to . . . Good-bye, Mrs. Gaines."

Mrs. Gaines surmised that Miss Kneed cared more about Mr. Forest than she had thought. "Good! Because he has a really good business going over there."

Lily spent the time she was used to spending with Weldon musing, thinking. About all the things that had happened to her in the last year. All the changes in her life. About her past, her mother, and Maddy.

"I used to feel so guilty because I was born ugly. I wondered who my father was because no one else in my family looked like me. I thought I would be set apart from the whole world all my life, until I died. Because I was ugly. My whole life was a wasteland of ugliness . . . and loneliness. I had made a gift of my life, my future, to my mother . . . and Maddy. Now . . . look what Weldon has done for me. He changed my . . . No, he helped me change my life. I work hard. Thank God for self-preservation."

In the past year, she had thought with all her business activity, school, all the new things in her life, she would never be lonely again. She had been almost drunk with all the things she was discovering about life. "And it is, at last, my life. I exist; I am real."

After the first few days of Weldon not being around, a different kind of loneliness moved into her apartment with her. She had not acquired many new things, except for the things Weldon brought or sent to her. At last, she was able to buy as many books as she wanted. She now had a fine library in the second bedroom.

One empty evening, after browsing through her "library," she found nothing that interested her. She felt the loneliness move close, inside her, again. Right in her lovely apartment, right inside the expensive silk negligee lovingly covering her body. It surprised her when the thought came into her head, "I'm not satisfied. I'm still lonely. I need some . . . thing."

She sighed as she sipped from her glass of wine. "What more

can I need? Is it love I am missing? They say you can't miss what you've never had. And I don't miss all that love music by Cole Porter, Dinah Washington, and Frank Sinatra. And all those Billie Holiday songs he loves to play all the time. I love music, but that stuff makes you want to haul off and kiss somebody, anybody."

She set the glass down. "Do I love Weldon? No, I know I don't love Weldon. But I do love Weldon...in some..." She reached for the wineglass. "I miss Weldon; I need Weldon. So . . . I must love him. But, I thought there was supposed to be fireworks, bells, a certain feeling." She finished the bottle of wine before she went to bed.

Lily Bea had told herself, after Maddy, she never wanted to make love, have sex, again in her life. "At least, not for a long, long time." She knew she felt something for Weldon, but . . . was it love? The next day, at work in the shop, she thought, "Wouldn't I know?" What she did know was that she was extremely lonely, and worried about Weldon.

Everywhere she turned her eyes, something made her think of him. In fact, she constantly thought of him. "Did I hurt his feelings? Was he just asking for a closer friendship? No, he said he loved me. Loved me? What can this wealthy white man want with me? If it was that, sex, why didn't he just say it a long time ago? No, it can't be sex. He didn't say that. I know we are friends, close friends. Wouldn't sex mess it up? Lord, I don't know nothing at all. But, what am I going to do? Should I leave? No! I have a job! And a business down on paper. To hell with all this love shit! Oh,

Mama!" But she began to huddle back inside herself again. Being without Weldon.

Lily didn't think she was in love with anyone, but she hated her loneliness. The loneliness she seemed to be making for herself.

She did not want a sexual life with him, or anyone. But she wanted possession of him, and was possessive of him already. She wanted someone she could give what she could give, without anything being really taken from her. She was afraid of failure, of his really seeing her; she was afraid of being ugly again.

She faced her own truths. Thinking, "I haven't really given him anything for all he has given me. The money the shop makes could be *all* his. He's already wealthy. I have given him nothing, really." She took another sip of her wine (she was sipping quite a bit of wine lately). After a moment, she asked herself, "What was it I wanted? What did I think I would have to do for what I wanted?" Another sip, and she thought, "Why . . . I wanted to be free. Well, I'm free. But when someone wants to love you, and they have given you your freedom . . . How do you keep your freedom at the same time you give yourself up?" Her mind was in turmoil.

Weldon hadn't been out of town. He had gone to a golf tournament, left early, gone home, and stayed at home. He was a little worn from a few sleepless nights and useless, boring days. Otherwise he was resigned to his life without the hope of Lily Bea. He reasoned, "She is a good businesswoman. Nothing need change, and I'll still enjoy seeing her even if I can't have her closer to me. She's almost my only joy."

He was self-conscious when he stopped by the Flower Cleaners. He opened the door, trying to smile, but his heart was sad. Then he looked up to see Lily hastening toward him. Her eyes were bright with warm welcome. She was saying, "We've missed you, Mr. Forest! I'm so glad to see you're back." She held her hands out to grasp his, then she remembered they were in the shop, and quickly changed to a handshake.

His heart immediately lifted. He thought, "The look in her eyes doesn't mean she is changing her mind, or that she loves me, but her feelings are sincere." When he was leaving, he said, "Later, you can fill me in on everything." His spirit had lifted. He stepped lighter for the rest of the day.

That evening when he went by Lily's place, he didn't put on any love songs, he played some Erik Satie they both liked. They had their usual glass of wine and talked. She didn't want to seem forward, but she hugged him anyway. They slipped back into their usual ways. But now, she hugged him when he left to go home.

Days passed and they slipped back into their comfortable routine. She noticed, though, he never played his romantic music anymore. He never played any music. She would put something on the record player herself because she wanted him pleased when he was with her.

The days also brought her to the knowledge that she had the need *to* love, as well as her lifelong desire to *be* loved. Weldon had become someone she could share her joys with, her enthusiasms, and her sad moments. And her business, he was integral to that.

At one point, she thought, "I could open my own business . . . for myself. I have money." After only a few moments she realized Weldon Forest was the impetus for her success. The location, the clientele, the very atmosphere of success. "And it is him, him, him, who has made my whole life so good, so full, so wonderful, so new, so grand. He really cares about me." She sipped. "Then why am I so lonely?"

She thought another minute or two, then said, "I better go see my friend. I need help."

Then, she came to see me.

Lately, Lily Bea always looked really good when I saw her. We seldom saw each other, we usually talked on the telephone. This day, she was wearing a black dress beneath a camel-hair coat. When I helped her remove it, that coat was as soft as a cloud.

I fixed a little pot of green tea, so we could sit down and talk. She was fidgety, nervous. But she settled down as she told me the latest developments in her life. When she had brought me up-to-date, I asked her, "What do you really feel about Weldon? This man?"

She fooled around with her fingers a minute, then said, "I could say, I love him, as a friend."

"You could?"

"I do love him, as a friend." She took a deep breath, and said, "He is a white man. A *white* man, my friend."

I couldn't help it, I had to say it. "Almost everybody in the world talks about how God created everything and everybody. Yet, as soon as the time comes to act like it, they act like some people are better than some other people. God likes good people, not colors, Lily Bea. The way you talk about that man, he is a good man, don't care what color he is."

She was looking dead in my face. She smiled at me.

I asked her, "How do you think he feels about you, Lily Bea?"

"He never makes me feel any color at all. I feel . . . I know he loves me as a friend."

"He seems to want more than a friendship, Lily."

"That's why I'm here. I don't know what to do, and you are my friend."

"I can't tell you what to do with your body."

Lily tilted her head at me, saying, "What makes you think of my 'body'? I didn't say anything about a body."

"Well, what's left? When friendship is not enough? What else could you be thinking about, Lily Bea?"

"Well, I wanted you to help me with my mind."

So I just said what she didn't want to think of. "Well, when is the last time you made love? Not sex with Maddy; love!"

Lily Bea sighed, and dropped her shoulders, said, "Maddy is the only man I've ever known . . . that way."

"Well, Lily, that sex wasn't nothing bout no 'love.' You've never really been loved. Don't feel funny bout that; some women been married four or five times, have never really been loved. But, we're talking about you, now."

"I know. But, people say white men can't make love; so I still wouldn't know about being loved. And Weldon is married. I don't want . . . It's adultery."

"Weldon's adultery. Your fornication. And don't ever listen to what people say when they include 'everybody' of any color. I'm not going to tell you how I know, cause that would be telling you somebody else's business. But some white men are what is called a mighty good thing! And some black men are not! Human beings are all relative in their doings. Some is, and some ain't.

"Lily Bea, is it the 'feeling' that you are thinking of, or are you trying to be perfect? No one is, you know."

She started to say, "But——"

I interrupted, "If you been thinking about the 'feeling' you must have the desire. You've made love to that man already in your mind." She was shaking her head no. I just kept talking.

"I ain't smart enough to fix your life. You got to choose for yourself. But, me? I'd quit every other sin I was living, and do just one. I'd make love to a good clean man who means me all the good in the world, is not going to tear me down, is not a bum on the street, is not a crook, or a freak. Don't lie to yourself and don't make excuses. God knows, this is life and it ain't easy to live. Do right and you'll live better, with God's help. Do wrong, and you're on your own.

"At least He knows you have given it more thought than a whole heap of people in this world. But, don't set out to fool God. Don't test Him. Right or wrong, everything has consequences no matter what you decide to do.

"I don't know what to tell you, chile, but life is life. And you don't know no more now than you did when you first came in here. Cause a person can't tell another person what to put between them and their God. You have to talk to God bout that. Your heart is full of love and sincerity. God likes love and sincerity."

Lily Bea looked at me a long time. We talked a bit more about family things. She had bought that house her mother lived in for her mother, but kept it in her own name. It was the only way to control her mother's greedy begging. She didn't want to be around her mother, but that was still her mother and she could afford to buy that ole house.

Then she left with her head tucked down in her coat collar. My heart went with her because it's hard to live in this world sometime. Always making choices. Satan's busy, chile!

As hard as Lily's life had been, she had been a good girl, and a good woman. I could almost see what her humanness would lead her to do. Not quite, but almost. Cause she was dealing with someone who loved her and proved it. Love, real love, is strange and strong. She had a little fight going on in her mind.

Otherwise it would have to be her godliness, and a very, very few people got godliness in em. Very, very few. They are the blessed. I envy them, as I try to be one of them. There are so many temptations on this earth these days. I'm glad I'm older, and they are not in my face and neither my heart. Anymore.

Their business relationship and their friendship continued on smoothly. He was a gentleman, never touching her too much, or pressing his desires on her. Lily Bea was grateful, because her mind was still trying to make itself up. Then something happened to get both Weldon and Lily upset. Actually, Lily Bea was kind'a pleased.

The jeweler next door to the Flower Cleaners, Mr. Jacob, adored Lily. All his wife's clothes were, now, cleaned at least twice before they were even worn.

One morning Mr. Jacob came into the cleaners holding out his hand, which had a small jewelry box in it. The shop was empty. He asked Lily, "May I give you this pair of earrings, my dear Lily? They seem to be made for you! It would do my heart pleasure to see these adorn your face when I come in."

He opened the little box for her; two medium-sized, gorgeous diamonds were in each earring. They sparkled brilliantly as she smiled and reached for them. "Ohhhhh, Mr. Jacob! For me? Why would you want to give me such an expensive, beautiful set of earrings? You barely know me."

The smile in his old face was almost as brilliant as the diamonds. "Oh, but you see, as a jeweler, I know where such stones belong. These belong on you. Make an old man happy and accept them . . . as a friendship gift."

His face alternated, with his feelings, between sorrow and joy. She would refuse on one hand, and reach for them on the other. He would not take no for an answer; nor would he accept any payment arrangement. At last, she said, "All right, Mr. Jacob, I accept your friendship gift." He was happy as he grinned, patted her ear, and left her shop with a young, jaunty step.

In the following weeks she refused to accept any other gifts from Mr. Jacob. He wasn't angry; he just liked to come in her shop, see, and listen to her. Weldon, thoughtfully, watched the interplay.

He thought, briefly, of leaving his wife. He couldn't because she was his wife, and he had loved her. Did love her. "She has done me no wrong." He turned in a different direction.

Weldon bought Lily Bea a lovely Autumn Haze full-length mink coat. "I have accepted all your kindnesses, Weldon, and it's beautiful, you know it is. But I can't accept this coat. It's too much, it's too much."

He had an answer prepared. "Well, we are, at least your shop, is going to expand its services. We are going to start cleaning and storing furs. You need to have one; it is part of advertisement." He hung it in one of her closets. She didn't argue, she left it there. Some evenings, when he had gone, she took it out, put it on, and slept in it.

Weldon Forest was planning to attend a conference of clothing specialists. He wanted Lily Bea to go with him. His travel consultant made all the arrangements for the both of them. They flew to New York, and registered in one of the best hotels. His room did not adjoin hers; for Lily Bea's comfort their rooms were separated by one room in between. He smiled as he said, "So we can be close enough to talk about what we learn without walking the length of this hotel!"

He was still a gentleman, but he touched her hands more. Pressed his warm hand upon her back as he steered her to seats at dinner tables and the auditorium. After dinner the first night, he kissed her good night on her forehead at the door of her room. When he complimented her on some observation she made, he hugged her, saying, "I love you, Lily Bea."

On their second evening, he took her for a walk on the busy streets of New York. She was enthralled with the sights and his voice as he guided her. On their return, as they were reaching the hotel he began talking to her, seriously.

"Lily, I'm not going to watch my words tonight. I know, you know, I love you. I want you. I have wanted you for a long, long time. Forever, it seems. I know you don't love me, at least I don't think you do." He held her hand tighter a moment, as he anticipated her fear.

"No, you don't have to do anything you don't want to do. I wouldn't enjoy that anyway. Nothing between us would change; it would only be better. If you do not want me, in that way, I will stop 'hanging' around you like I do. I will stop being ridiculous, making a fool of myself and bothering you. But . . . I want you to know, I love you, and I want you."

Lily Bea didn't know what to say. She was alarmed, and confused about their life together. She did have a love for him. She didn't want to hurt him. She went up in the elevator with these thoughts, and more, on her mind. "It's not him I don't want; it's sex. I don't want to go through sex again. Ever."

They reached her room, where he turned her body to face his. He said, "Lily, I'm not telling you to do anything you don't want to do. But, tonight . . . I am going to go to my room, get into my bed, and wait. I am going to leave my door unlocked. If you decide to come to me, I will be happy. If you do not decide to come to me, I will understand. Remember, I love you."

He opened her door with her key, gave it back to her, and went down the hall to his room. He hadn't looked back.

Lily Bea took a bath, then sat by her windows, looking down at the busy avenue. She sighed, sat back, looking up at the sky. She sat there for an hour or so, at last turning to stare at her bed.

Then she got up, looked down at her pretty, pale green nightgown. She put her robe on, picked up her key, opened her door, and went out. She stood outside the door a moment, glad the hall was empty. She looked toward Weldon's room for another moment or two. Slowly, she began walking toward his room. Her heart was pounding with trepidation as she stood facing his door.

She turned the knob lightly, with a hesitant hand; the door was unlocked and opening. Unaware, she took a deep breath, she pushed the door, softly, open wider. She stepped over the threshold, closing the door behind her. There was no light except for a muffled light from beyond the window coverings. The faint sound of music, a love song, softly floating, caressed the air around her.

There was enough light to see his form in the bed. Waiting. He didn't say anything; he didn't even sigh. He waited. Lily moved closer to the empty side of his bed. The cover was already turned down, waiting for her.

In the darkness, soundlessly, he made his first movement; he stretched his arm across the pillows to her. He didn't raise his arm to encourage her; his arm held no question. He laid his arm open and down on the bed. Where he wanted her body to lie. And waited.

Lily let her silken robe slide down from her body to the floor. She slipped into the bed, laid her head on his arm, and closed her eyes. She felt calm, but her heart was beating so hard.

She was expecting the greedy, grasping, rough hands of Maddy.

Seeming to barely touch her, Weldon placed his other arm around her waist; the arm under her head gently drew her body close, closer. Slowly and gently, his hand moved over her body over her breasts, to her thighs, her hips. She felt encircled by him. She liked the faint aroma filling her nostrils. Nothing jarred her senses. She relaxed more.

He was taking her out of her world, completely, into a new world she had not ever dreamed of. Love, kindness, and tenderness. She had read about it, but those were fairy tales to her. Not really true.

She had not noticed when he placed his thigh across her hips. At the same time he placed his cheek on her cheek, gently nudging her face toward his. Their lips touched with the slightest pressure; he remained still as he held her so close, so close. Subtly his tongue caressed her lips, opening them, moving warmly, slowly, over her lips, into her mouth.

Suddenly, she was calm. The gentle experience of the kiss, the gentle tongue, exerting no pressure or demand, filled her body with a sweetness new to her. She could even feel her eyeballs, beneath her closed eyelids, widen with excitement. He raised his body up, over her, looking down at her. He rested on his elbow as he removed her nightgown, one shoulder at a time. He pushed it, still gently, down her body to her feet, and off.

He moved atop her and just lay there, two or three minutes, feeling her. He was in no rush. She could feel every nerve in her body, wakening, demanding. Suddenly a hungry, starving body.

Deliberately slow, he kissed her body from her lips down to her feet, then kissed them as he moved, returning, to her lips. Resting his head, along the way, on the rough-soft, curling hair of her private body. He continued his journey, stroking, kissing. He looked, in wonder, at his dream. "This is the warm, beautiful body I have longed for."

Lily Bea placed her arms above her head, and stretched her body, to the new and thrilling experience. She had thought she would want to escape him, "after." Now she knew she wanted to remain just where she was, in this new world with him. Time, fear, the world, everything was gone, stripped away from her by the gentle hands of Weldon.

Lily wanted to feel him enter even her heart. It opened; he was turning her into a flower. The bed became enchanted, the magic carpet. As he kissed her throat, and placed his knee between her loose thighs, strange sounds of rushing water filled her head. Like an ocean's roar. The flower she was now unfolded even more. Her body stretched, again, of its own free will.

As he lay on her, over her throbbing heart, she had a fleeting thought, "He is not even heavy." He didn't have to open her legs or search; her body was ready, it opened to accept him. She felt the hair on his chest on her breast; little flames touched her muscles, her bones.

Then she felt the tender monster enter her stomach; opening her flower completely, bringing body-music into her soul. Weldon's caresses soothed, even as they awakened all the places on her body and in her soul that Maddy had dragged into only pain, leaving wounds. Weldon was healing them all.

Swiftly, briefly, Lily Bea thought of golden apples, and flying carpets. Weldon performed the magic simplicity of making love, love. He stopped, briefly, now and then, lying soaked and buried in the flower of her body; until she would make a sobbing sound, and moving her body, would force him to move with her, again. She sang a new song as he moved over her, a little light opera. It was the first time a woman had sung, lying beneath him. It was a sound he heard in his mind, and thrilled to, over and over for the rest of his life.

That was how Weldon carried Lily Bea on a magic carpet. Ever so tenderly, and gently, over the edge, into another world of new golden apples. Dear reader, what more could you wish to know about that night?

From that time on, Weldon had neonlike lights glowing from his body that no one else could see.

And, for Lily Bea, the body she thought she hated had turned into a garden of delight and wonder.

From that time on, when Weldon came to her house, Lily was the one who put the romantic music on the record player. She had added Barry White, Dinah Washington, Ray Charles, Aretha

Franklin, Nat "King" Cole, and a few others. Lily Bea thought, "I must be in love."

When Weldon and Lily returned home from their New York conference, their evenings were different, closer. The business relationship remained the same, running smoothly. He gave Lily another quarter of the business. Now she owned seventy-five percent and he owned twenty-five percent.

Lily Bea even seemed prettier to herself.

Other changes occurred, though. Now, when he took her out to dinner they went to very nice, but dimly lighted, out-of-the-way places. It couldn't have been any shame of his; he had never cared about "other people" before.

He also became very jealous. He even wanted her to stop Mr. Jacob, the jeweler, from stopping by to talk to her so regularly. A year or so passed in this manner.

Now, something had been in the back of Lily's mind for some time. She didn't see many Black people in her life, and she wanted to. She went back to the community college to check for anyone who was learning her business. There were only two Black people there: a man thirty-three years old, and a woman twenty-four years old. They promised to stop in to see her when their knowledge had progressed enough to have something to offer her.

Around that time, Mr. Jacob, loving Lily, in his way, was influenced by her color, the rich brown. So when his assistant became ill and had to be replaced, he asked around among his fellow jewelers for information of a Negro man, or woman, to fill the vacancy. There was only one: a half Jewish, half Negro man, Sol Morris. He was in his early thirties, had been raised in the craft, and wanted to make a move from the East. New York, to be exact.

There was an interview, and after Mr. Jacob was satisfied he wouldn't have a crook on his hands around his diamonds, he hired the young man. Well, crooks come in all colors, you know, rich or poor.

Sol was about five feet nine inches tall, weighing about one hundred sixty pounds. He was serious about his future, possessing a fair education. His father had not married his mother, but paid enough attention to his son to help him, now and again. His father had suggested Sol go into the field of gemstones and jewelry making.

Sol found gemology interesting and absorbing. He enjoyed the brilliant lights and colors of gems. He was a quiet man, never married or wanting to get married. He took his women on the run. Only one or two women made a sound enough impression on him to make him consider marriage. But he was unable to support a woman, and perhaps a child at this time. He remained single.

Sol had worked for Jacob a couple of months when Lily came in for some jewelry repair. He did not think anything special about her. He liked the sound of her voice, but thought she was unattractive. "She is smart, though; she is managing a business."

Lily Bea noticed Sol because he was a Black man working with jewelry. They talked. "Well, I hope you enjoy our little city, Mr. Morris."

"I already do," he answered, "I just have to find my way around to the bookstores, the theatre, and museums."

Lily smiled. "Well, if you need any help, I'll be glad to help you. I can tell you the two best bookstores right now. I'll make a little list for you for the other things." Later she gave him the list, then they both forgot about each other in their busy lives.

Being an observant man, Sol became acquainted with the Flower Cleaners. He asked Mr. Jacob, "That is not her business, is it, Mr. Jacob?"

Mr. Jacob dusted off the counter as he thought a moment. "Hmmm, I think it is; but it is also his, Weldon Forest's. I don't know their agreement."

Sol noticed that Mr. Jacob's face lit up when Lily passed by the store or her name was brought up. That Mr. Jacob visited the cleaners at least once a day. It amused Sol. He liked his boss.

By the time six months had passed Sol felt the presence of Lily. She was kind; she had helped him find a decent apartment at a decent rent. Her voice charmed him. Her shy smile charmed him, also. He noticed that Weldon Forest was often near Lily or the business.

Sol liked the way Lily dressed, and her gracefulness. Pretty soon she was not ugly to him, and his face lit up when he saw her. But love was far from his mind. He was working and saving. He wanted his own shop. He noticed neither shop had many Black customers. But he also knew they dealt in a better quality of things than the shops he had worked at in New York.

On his days off he walked over new sections of the city he

had moved to. He sat in parks with his pen, designing jewelry he knew he would never make. But, he thought, "Who knows?"

He grew lonely. One day his landlady had a couple of black kittens she was planning to take to the SPCA, but was afraid they would be put to sleep. In his loneliness he decided to take one; immediately he thought of Lily Bea, for some reason, and took the other kitten to give to her. He named his kitten Rain.

He took a large, pretty box from the jewelry store, and put the kitten in it. Thinly wrapped it, and took it to Lily. She looked at the wobbling box questioningly. Pleased with the surprise, she unwrapped the box. She smiled and gasped, "Ohhhhhhh," at the cute, little black kitten and pressed it to her breast. "I wonder why I never thought of a pet for all my lonely times." Lily looked up as she named her kitten Shadow. She saw Weldon standing in the doorway looking at her and Sol. He stood watching a moment, then he frowned.

Soon Shadow had everything a good kitten needs. Lily enjoyed it more than she had imagined. Who knew? Weldon often watched her stroke the kitten, and wished she would stroke the mink coat he had given her. "I didn't know you wanted a pet," he said.

Weldon did not like Sol Morris, but there was nothing to be done about the friendship. He couldn't ask Jacob to fire Sol; he knew Jacob would refuse because he liked Lily Bea himself.

To make matters worse for Weldon, his wife became ill. At first it was nothing to worry about, but as time passed, and she didn't get well, he became more concerned about his wife of such a long time. His son flew in to see about his mother; he left when the doctor said, "It will just take time, she will be all right." But, Mrs. Forest did not look well at all. Weldon began to spend more time with her, most of his days, and many of the evenings he used to spend with Lily Bea.

Lily Bea more than understood; she was pleased. "Weldon always does the right thing. He is a good man," she thought during her evenings with just Shadow to talk to.

As her time was spent more alone, Lily paid more attention to the different men that came in and out of her vision.

There was another Black man who came into the cleaning shop. He had special shirts he wanted done in a special way. He was a nice-looking man, Monte Gales, always smiling. He never said anything to Lily Bea that was in poor taste. He would smile and spend a few moments, if the shop was empty, to exchange a few words with her. He was a musician. Lily Bea had noticed there was no ring on his finger.

One day he said, "You know, I never see you at any club. Why? don't you like music?"

She smiled as she pulled the plastic over his shirts. "I don't know. I like music. I guess I just never think of going to a club to hear it. I have records."

He smiled back, showing nice, even white teeth, "Records are good. But, nothing beats live music. Why don't you come hear my group? I'll leave word at the door; be my guest. You'll enjoy yourself."

"I may do that, Mr. . . . ?"

"Monte, just call me Monte."

Weldon was there that day. He didn't like these developments. It wasn't just because they were Black men; they were men, single men. He told Lily Bea, "You have to be very careful in a club full of strangers, and every kind of person there is to try to avoid."

Lily didn't run out to the club, but as the days passed she thought more about it. She thought about both Sol and Monte. She wondered if Sol would like to go to the club with her. "But, Sol is very serious, and Monte is full of life and fun. Maybe I'll go by myself one night, at least I'll be Monte's guest, so I won't be a single woman out for anything but music."

Things were changing.

Weldon's wife needed him more. Lily was alone more. And when they were together, lovemaking didn't seem right, to either of them, with his wife at home sick.

One lonely evening, when Lily Bea was not expecting Weldon, she went to hear music, to laugh and talk, at the club. She needed her mood lifted. She called Sol and asked if he wanted to join her. He did. They had a really pleasant evening: a few drinks, and much good music, blues and light jazz.

When the evening was over Sol took her to her door. They were not at the cheek-kissing stage, they were saying "Good night" and "I had a good time" things. As she turned her key, opening the door, she saw Weldon sitting in the easy chair turned to face the door. His eyes were smoldering, but he looked calm.

Lily turned to thank Sol for bringing her home when Weldon said, "Go ahead, invite him in. Don't let me stop you. I'm leaving anyway." But he did not move to leave.

Lily was embarrassed that Sol should know her private business, and at Weldon's attitude. She said, "He isn't coming in. He only brought me home."

Weldon said, "Ah, but it's early."

Lily said, "It's late."

Weldon said, "Well . . ."

Lily said a final good night to Sol, and Sol left. She took her coat off as she said, "I didn't expect you, Weldon."

"Obviously."

"There is no reason to talk like I have done something wrong, Weldon. I was—"

Weldon interrupted her. "I do not want that man near this apartment again."

Lily, slightly surprised, said, "This is my apartment, Weldon. Sol and I are only friends."

He smirked. "Everyone is 'only friends' in the beginning."

Lily decided he was just stressed with his wife's illness and business. She walked to him, and put her arms around his neck.

Weldon made a mistake. He removed her arms, picked up his coat from the rack, opened the door, and started walking out. I can tell you, he expected her to stop him; but she didn't.

He could find no way to cover over the incident and go back inside. She looked confused, but she didn't get angry. She didn't do anything at all. Nothing but tilt her head, slightly smile, and slowly nod her head. With silence, time became strained. He sighed, and left closing the door quietly.

Their meetings became strained as well. Her thoughts circled around "There is no friend of mine he likes. He doesn't even like my cat. There is no one I can talk to, except customers on their way out of the shop door. I can't invite a friend to my home." Then she would think again. "Oh, God, forgive me; he helped me get everything I have. He is the reason my life has changed so much."

But, upon reflection, she would think, "I work. I work hard for my living. I have added to everything he gave me. I didn't turn into a problem for him. He hasn't lost anything; he has gained. He gave me what he gave me because he wanted something for himself." She shook her head. "Ohhh, I love him. But, he has a wife. I have no one except a man who has a wife. He has a son; I have no child at all. He is in his future. I am working for my future; and what is my future? I don't want to hurt him, but I have to decide my life for myself."

She talked on the phone to Monte, but she didn't go back to the club at that time. She didn't feel like "havin fun!" She remembered the words "Any fool can have some fun; you betta get you some sense in your life!" She continued working hard. At home, her company was the growing kitten Shadow.

She had more than enough money for one dream. She found a Realtor and they found a house. She paid down on a house of her own. "I'll invite whomever I want to invite. To *my* house!"

She furnished that house with everything new; decorated it to her taste. For the first time, for anyone in her family history, she had bought and could furnish her own house. "I ain't rentin!" She loved modern Italian and Mediterranean furniture, with some French influences.

When the house was completed to her satisfaction, she gave a dinner. A dinner for two. She served the best of everything she knew he liked. She invited Weldon Forest.

I'll say this for him, he was no longer angry; he was only sad and lonely. But he was proud for her, and of her. He was a good man. And when dinner was through they made good love to each other. When he left to go home where his wife needed him, he was satisfied. His stomach was pleased and full, his heart was pleased and full, his body was pleased. His mind was no longer teeming with worries about love. He did not know the affair was struggling in its last days. Somewhere in Weldon's mind, he thought they were making a new beginning. I guess you just have to wait and see.

Feeling good, and secure in her new life, her loneliness pressed her to invite her mother and sister over for dinner. It had taken three years for this decision. They had never been invited to her apartment. She had been afraid of what Weldon might see. She no longer cared.

Lily Bea was proud the day her family came to her house.

Her sister had brought her boyfriend because he had a car, a light blue, battered old Cadillac. They parked in the nice middle-class neighborhood, and got out of the car, making a lot of noise.

Their voices were loud, and their laughter held a sharp, hard edge in it.

They entered the neat brick house with a bit of fanfare about the yard. "She ain't buyin this house! She rentin!" Or, "I bet these people round here ain't never seen no real people before! I wonder does any Black people live round here! She always tryin to be more'n what she is!"

At last they were inside, coats removed, and drink in hand. They all got a little drunk, because this was free liquor, and you don't leave as long as there is some liquor still in a bottle. They had a good time trying to drag Lily Bea down.

They had a delicious dinner of some different food Lily Bea knew they didn't get much of, if any. Sorty, with her usual razor-sharp smile, asked, "Where the real food? I had my mouth all set for some ham hocks or pork chops! What you call this? A rib roast? I cook my ribs in the bar-b-que pit!"

The pretty sister said, "How you got that man to do all'a this for you? You must'a hoo-dooed him! Ain't nobody ever done nothin like this for me! Who'da thought a man id do all'a this for you! You even got a piano! You still tryin to play a piano?"

Sorty laughed as she said, "I go to church least once a month, and even God ain't helped me get a good house like you got your-self! You just got me that piece of junk I was already livin in!"

Through it all, finally Lily had them all settled at the table, grabbing over the food that looked so good. After they finished dinner Lily moved them into the living room. She was feeling pretty good, until she saw the boyfriend push Shadow off the couch, and kick the young startled cat out of his way. She picked Shadow up and held him in her lap.

Sorty, her mother, talked loud, cursing at times. For some reason she resented Lily Bea having more than she. "Girl, God knows you got nough room in this here house to bring your mama over here to live! God bless childrens who take care their mama! It's bout time you let us come round you! You always did ack like a fool.

"Sweetheart," she said, with that razor-sharp smile, "I don't need to go home to that ole piece of junk you done got for me! I need to live over here wit you! I bet I could even take care a house like this, keep it clean and all, but I ain't never had one." She sighed as she took another drink. "Some people just has all the luck!"

Her sister, who had laughed and teased her when they were young, watched her boyfriend stare at Lily Bea, the "ugly." Now her mean, ugly streak turned into something worse, mixed with self-pity and envy of Lily's success. She felt her hate for Lily as it filled her mind, heart, and stomach. She said, "I don't know how you lied yourself up on all this shit! I ain't even got no house at all. We all need to move over here!"

She smiled at her drunk boyfriend as she said, "You could come on over here to see me in your Candillac. Let these folks round here know we like nice things too!" She looked at Lily Bea, saying, "We like nice things too! We a family! We s'posed to stick together!"

Lily Bea listened as she moved around, cleaning up a broken dish or glass, wiping up their spilled drinks and food. She had planned to spend the evening with them, but now, she helped them get ready to leave.

They were going out the front door when Sorty said, "Well, now we know the way over here, we be comin back to see you."

Lily Bea, following them to their car to be sure they got in it and drove away, said, "No, don't come over here until I invite you. I mean that. I work. I am very busy. The police will be here if you come and I didn't invite you."

So they grumbled, cussed, and fussed, as they closed car doors, looking back at Lily Bea standing in front of that pretty brick house. Sister felt hate, Sorty felt cheated. The boyfriend just felt sick because he had tried to empty that bottle without eating much food.

Lily Bea went back, thankfully, into her house to clean it up. She petted Shadow. "I know you are glad they are gone, too." When she was putting things away she found three cigarette burns; one was long, as though the cigarette had been placed there and allowed to burn until it went out.

Lily Bea thought, "My golden apple has rotten spots. They don't ever need to come to my home again."

Loneliness always returns to some people when they don't have someone to share the things they enjoy. Lily found herself thinking of Sol and Monte.

Weldon visited, bewildered. Lily Bea was still a woman he loved; but life with her had become so complicated and confusing.

And the sex was over. He was a married man, and Lily wanted a future. She wanted a marriage of her own. What could he really offer her? She hadn't asked for his help when she bought her house. He was glad she had the house, but sorry he had not had a part in it. She had made his life happy. Now . . . a lot of his sunshine was gone; he carried an ache in his heart constantly.

Monte was a musician; she had never heard they were responsible people to marry. She knew he liked her, but he hadn't asked her to do more than hear his music. "He makes me laugh, and enjoy myself, though. He has never asked me to make love."

Sol had a future as a jeweler, but he didn't laugh enough, enjoy life enough. He was so serious. They talked economics and business often. He liked music, so they had quiet fun together. "He has never asked to make love to me.

"I have no real problems; just future problems. I'm coming along, though. I have peace, and God. I have nothing to be ashamed of in front of God anymore. And God will deliver me, I pray." Her other solution was to work harder as she prayed, "Deliver me, please, God."

One day, when a lady knocked on her door with Bible in hand, Lily Bea let her in; she was lonely. She wanted to talk. The lady became a regular visitor. Over time Lily Bea told the kind lady many of her private thoughts.

The lady told Lily, "You are young and foolish to think Beauty runs the world. If so, where is it? Beauty? It is in the eyes of the beholder. As a man thinks about others, so is he what he thinks of others. A person has to have some beauty in their self, to see the beauty in others which no one else may see. It never entered my mind that you were ugly. You are not ugly. Beauty is in the eyes of the beholder."

Lily Bea hugged those words to her breast, because they were true; they explained so much of her life to her.

Over the next year or so, both Monte and Sol became closer friends to Lily Bea. In time she learned they both wanted to make love to her. As good as her memories were of good lovemaking, she held herself back. She didn't really know why. "I'm not ready. Besides, I would choose Weldon because I know what kind of love he makes." But she didn't want to do that either.

Quite happily she had run into Robert Earner a few days ago. He had finished college several years ago, and was home to visit his family. He had married, had two children and a divorce. He seemed glad to see her. They talked about the old days at the Clean Cleaners. He had asked for her phone number, twice, before she gave it to him. She looked forward to his call.

She dreamed of traveling, ships and planes taking her exotic places. She had the money, and could take the time. But she hadn't done that yet either.

Shadow was grown, soft long fur, sweet and beautiful. And really was good company. They talked.

But, you know, loneliness was always just a thought away. One of those sad, lonely, rainy evenings, she sat in her living room with the fireplace burning. She was enjoying a glass of crisp white wine. Thinking. Lonely.

"Well, I guess I just have to prepare to be lonely." Sadly, she repeated, "I'm alone." She got up, fixed another glass of wine, and sat down to be sad again.

The house was bright, the music filling the rooms was mellow and good to her. The fire was bright. Shadow was stretched out, asleep, in front of it.

Another thought entered Lily Bea's mind. "I am alone," she smiled to herself, "but I'm in my own house." She sipped. "I have a business. I am not only alone; I am free. I may be ugly, but I have men who like me, might love me one day. I am alone . . . but . . . I am free!" She sipped a bit. "I have a little savings. I have a future, if I'm careful. I may be alone, but, thank God, I am free. I can make any decision, do within reason, whatever I want to do. All I have to do is work hard, take care of my own health, and live! And travel, go back to school for whatever I want and can afford. I am free. I didn't know this was where I was headed, but here I am . . . free!

"Thank You, God, thank You. You have delivered me."

She sat quietly enjoying her peace. The telephone rang. She frowned. But . . . she went to answer it. Someone was trying to reach her.

Success

This *Friday had* been a ghastly, dark, and dreary rainy day. All the people who had planned to venture out into the night life of the city frowned out through their windows at the water-soaked streets.

Some, a few who loved the rain, anticipated a long night at home. A golden, crackling fire burning in the fireplace, a good meal cooking on the stove, or relaxing with a good book or a good mate. They smiled upon the view through their windows and the sound of rain upon their roofs.

It was the night of the yearly big-band event at the cheaply glamorous Well Come Nite Club. Every dance lover had planned to go, from scholarly professionals to the out-of-work who could afford the door charge and one drink.

As she talked on the telephone, attorney Tashyah Tillsdal looked through her oversized bay windows at the gray skies, disgustedly. Anxiety and disappointment showed on her very well-cared-for face. She had no complacent thought as she viewed her drenched lawn and the large dripping trees.

Tashyah, a single woman, had passed the bar examination three years earlier. In such a short time, she had done well for herself as legal representative for a few very important corporations.

She had had plans for the night, and was saying on the phone, "I had so looked forward to this special night of dancing, laughter, and fun at the Well Come Club. I know the club is a little beneath me. Nevertheless, so many different types of dancers congregate there. Black, white, red, brown, and tan people. No matter what type of music they play, jazz, rock and roll, blues, Latin rhythms, Caribbean, swing, rap, whatever, there is someone there who knows how to do it! And do it good!"

She listened a moment, then, "Even when there is no live music, the DJ is really hip and cool, with a broad spectrum of music to choose from."

She listened, now and again, naturally.

"Well, I do love my home, but I've had it at least a year now. And, when I can, I get up on my days off and light my fireplace. I put on my music. I usually order in Chinese or pizza, and all that jazz. But . . . I get bored." She checked her manicure as she listened.

"Well . . . but it's not enough. There's nothing to do after the fire is lit, and I've had my cup of tea, glass of wine, or diet drink, my order-in dinner; then what? After work, there's just me. Alone."

She listened with a frown. Then said, "Well, I do want a man, but I don't want one of these self-centered, debt-ridden, boring, can't make love asses. Who's to want? . . .

"Married!?" She laughed a little. "Well, I do love him; I did, anyway. But I'm only twenty-seven and these nineteen- and twenty-year-olds give up so much ass and head, he didn't have enough time to get to know all my perfect ways." She laughed, then grew serious. "I have more serious things on my mind than sex anyway."

She listened a moment, thoughtfully, then said, "Well, you know. A man has to come up to my expectations. It is not easy to find and get a woman like I am: educated, well-read, looks good, dresses extremely well, and looks extremely good in my clothes!" She laughed at her own immodesty, but she meant it.

"Yeah, girlfriend, you said it! And a hot good body very well taken care of . . . yes!" She rose up to look out of the window again. "Well, this mess is still pouring down." She relaxed back on the sofa. "I'm tired of sitting in this house all by myself doing nothing! Maybe someone, my dream man, might be there tonight. Yours too!"

She listened as she sat up again, "Well . . . let's go anyway! The men of both of our dreams may be there tonight. It feels like a magic night to me." In a moment, "Say what?"

An answer, "I don't know about you, but I am a young woman. Twenty-seven is not old. My clock has many, many years to tick. Speak for yourself!" She took a sip of her drink and lay back to relax again.

"Girlfriend, it is said that men look over a good woman to get to all those freebee females out there who slobber for a man; no class, no manners, and no education, obviously. Lay on their backs and do anything in bed! Freaks! That's why I don't want you to bring your friend Betta, because men get wrapped up in her looks that say 'I'll do anything for you, and do it tonight!' " She listened a moment, then said, "I looooove myself, honey, and some man better do himself a favor and get me while he can. . . .

"Well, a man has to work to get me. That's why I'm not married. A man has to show me something! I've worked hard to create myself. I am no passing fancy; I am the real thing! Don't take me lightly! No, no. As James Brown, or was it Jesse Jackson, used to say, 'I am Somebody!' " She laughed with her friend. "Of course you are!"

The laughter ended and Tashyah got serious. "Well, let's get dressed and go anyway. I'm not afraid of a little water falling from the heavens!" She looked down, briefly, to check her pedicure. "Okay, a lot of water." She checked her watch. "All right! I'll meet you there at eleven." She shook her finger at the telephone as she said, "Don't you change your mind, Shirla!"

They said their good-byes, and she put the phone down as she said, "Silly bitch. Stay home and curl up with a good book indeed! If I curl up, it won't be with a book! No wonder her man keeps two or three other women."

Tashyah sat still, feeling the silence of her house for several moments, quietly thinking, as she looked through her blurry windows.

Then she said, aloud, from some deep empty place in her soul, "Oh God, oh God. I am so lonely! All this big beautiful house, and the only problem is, it is empty! No one is 'home' except me." Her mind mused as the rain pelted the windows, echoing her words.

Her mind clicked back to the moment. "But I can't find a man sitting at home with a book! Not even the Bible! Which reminds me; I'm supposed to call my mother to let her know if I'm going to church with her or not. Well, I'm not going; ain't no man, for me, sitting in any church. So I don't want to talk to her. I need a man's love, not God right now! I don't care how good she thinks they may be!"

She checked her wristwatch again, and looked at the lovely clock on the mantel of the fireplace. "Three whole hours to wait." She sighed. "It won't take me more than one hour to get ready. I'll just have another drink."

So she sat alone, and listened to her music, sad blues music. All secure in her bank account, her profession, and her beautiful home. All alone.

Now, we all know there is nothing wrong with being alone, it is a desirable thing. And there is a time for everything. But the time of aloneness, peace, has to be what you want.

Now, it happened that way across the city, in another upper-class suburb, there was a young man named Gregory "Greg" Holes. Greg was widely considered a fine youngish man, still in his thir-

ties. All his school days behind him, he was a successful op-
tometrist.

He, too, was alone, standing in front of his living room windows with drink in hand, thinking. "Stormy weather. Well, if I
go out driving, I'm not wearing any of my best shoes in this
mess." He sipped his drink, musing. "I ought to call Lawanta . . .
or Betty, for some good conversation."

He laughed a little as he turned from the window. "Kula
won't take me back in for the night, I know that. What's wrong
with these women anyway? They want the sex, but they want some
kind of commitment . . . and I'm not about to get tied up in that
shit. Once was enough! Nuba was enough! She thought I was too
tied up in myself. Self-centered, she said. Well, what the hell else is
better to be tied up with?"

He prepared another drink for himself. A strong drink. He
was thinking of his college and football days. "All the girls you
could want. Everywhere! The cast is cut down now, though. There
ain't nothing out there that's good enough for me." He took a long
swallow. "You look into eyes and there is nothing but emptiness
there." He stood in front of the mirror awhile, silently thinking,
not seeing the emptiness in his own eyes.

Greg knew about the dance at The Club, and he knew he was
going to go. He was tired of his comfortable, masculine house, so
richly furnished in a style that loudly proclaimed "A man lives
here!"

He did not let women leave handkerchiefs or purses, earrings, or anything "by accident." "Not here! This is mine. All for me. Yours truly!" He smiled at himself. "No, you leave your stuff at your own house . . . if you have one! These women are too dumb to have a house, they'd rather have a fur coat and a Mercedes. Or anything, rather than something sensible. Little, beautiful, lusty fools!!"

He chuckled as his thoughts continued. "BUT some of them are pretty, with nice, plump, smooth, rounded behinds, so . . . I guess I'm going to the dance, out in all this rain, and see what I can catch. No need to wear anything special; most of them at that club don't know the difference anyway. They can just look at me, the man inside the clothes! My aunt is always trying to tell me I'm missing something if I don't find God's love, first. But, she can't see all I do have!"

Later, he did take the extra time and attention for his clothes. He was a vain man, just like vain women. And he had hopes he didn't admit to, even to his own self, because he was a cool player. Still . . . he was alone. After all, you can only look at yourself in your many mirrors just so long. And . . . it does not banish loneliness. You may love yourself, but you were really made to love someone else. And Love don't love nobody, they say.

When he left his house, he ran carefully with his body bent to escape the splattering drops, to his Mercedes that was parked in his long driveway. As he turned the key, the motor gently roared like a well-taught lion. He was thinking, "Who knows, maybe that one woman will be there in the crummy club, after all." He drove his flaming red, shining automobile into the night through the falling rain, flashing through the streets, looking through his windows to see if anyone would see him.

Reaching the club, Greg parked his automobile, very carefully, far away yet close enough for the lights to discourage thieves seeing that flashing red, beautiful car. Moments later, car keys casually jingling in his hand, he stood coolly, with his back to the bar, looking over the brilliant scene. Ceiling lights flashed to their own rhythms as the music blared. It was early, only ten o'clock or so. Rap was blasting out and into every corner, over and under everything in the room. Later, they would slow the music; play more bluesy-type, slow-dragging, funky music for those who wanted to grow closer before the night ended.

Greg smiled at the nearly packed crowd. Smiled as he surveyed and rated everyone his good eyes fastened upon.

Tashyah and Shirla parked and made their way hastily through the rain to the crowded entry of The Club. They stood a moment inside the door, shaking and brushing the rain away, removing their hats. They searched for the best place to sit among the crowded tables. The man who had taken their entry money leaned over to signal to a waitress, pointing at the lovely ladies. He smiled at them as he turned back to his job. "Near the dance floor!" Tashyah hollered to the waitress. Once seated, they, too, surveyed the room for likely dancers or . . . people they knew.

Greg, also watching the door, had seen the two women come

in. Not much time passed before Greg caught Tashyah's eye as she was taking a sip of her drink. She liked what she saw. She leaned close to Shirla, and nodded in his direction. "That one sure is a fine specimen of a man. Oooh wee! And that sports jacket! Three hundred dollars, if it was a dime! Look to see if he is still looking at me, at us." She did not nudge Shirla; that was for schoolgirls to do. And you shouldn't show other people what you may want for yourself. Shirla was finding her own anyway.

Tashyah could watch someone from the corner of her eye and see everything around her. That was one of the things that made her a good lawyer. She kept Greg in her sight.

Then, someone asked her to dance and she hopped up, gladly. She danced toward the bar so whoever "he" was he could see her and her smooth dance steps and body language. She could shake her booty with the best of them; well, almost.

Watching him, furtively, she saw him see her again, and was glad she had worn the almost see-through blouse, which she almost hadn't worn on the rainy night. The last note sounded, and she flashed him a quick, titillating smile as she turned to make her way through the crowd, back to her seat.

Greg liked her style of dance and her body. But he thought her blouse was a cheap effort. He did like what he saw, though. When her partner walked away from her, he knew she was alone. He decided to watch her awhile, as well as two other ladies he had tabbed. After all, he may be a "lonely" man, but he thought "single" man was a better word for him. And, there were seven days in a week. Plenty of time, for everybody, in time.

Finally, there was only one hour before closing time. Greg had checked out the other two women in conversations; one was too nosy, and the other thought she was funny and witty, unsuccessfully. He discarded them and decided to ask Tashyah to dance.

Tashyah thought she knew exactly what he had been doing all the while. So when he started toward her, she became involved in pretend-deep conversation with Shirla. Disturbing Shirla and her new friend she was trying to talk with.

Like a gentleman, he asked her for a dance. The music was slow. The DJ knew what his job was. He had two or three females hanging around his own corner. As Greg and Tashyah melted into each other's arms, they smiled. Their bodies felt good together.

After that dance, Greg, holding Tashyah's hand, found an empty space where they could, at least, be alone to talk. He wanted to talk to this woman with the hot body.

Now he knew she was an attorney. They danced and talked over three more drinks each. Among other things, Greg told Tashyah she was a perfect fit in his arms. "This could work, baby." And his favorite line, "I only have eyes for you."

Tashyah was flattered. She had held her head back, looking up into his face, with all the interest and beauty she could. She flashed her looks, smiled shyly or innocently or invitingly or admonishingly as his words might demand, while he looked down on her with delight. His eyes holding hers, he talked smoothly in his best voice about his accomplishments and a few made-up dreams and goals.

"I'm not married, but I really want a good wife and a few

kids . . . a son." He thought he was jiving, but he was telling the truth and didn't know it.

Tashyah almost shared her desires. "I do, too. I want to be married, and make a good home for a family. But there seems so little to choose from." She had told the truth. "I'm not in any hurry, though. I have a very satisfying life." She lied.

He had already told her she was the most beautiful woman there . . . and she believed him because she thought so, too.

They were loath to part when the club was closing, emptying out. So she clung to his hand, casually. He didn't want to be alone, so he let her cling to his hand while he clung back.

Shirla and her friend caught up with Tashyah and told her they were ready to go. When Greg found out she was riding with Shirla, he said to her, "Come ride with me. I'm safe, ask my secretary." That was for Shirla's benefit. He continued, "It's too early to go home. Let's go to breakfast, Tashyah."

She answered, "A marvelous idea! I'm starved."

As they had the late night, early morning breakfast, they talked. In the clear bright lights he saw she was really quite attractive. And he remained really handsome to her. They could have fallen in love. They were, both, potentially good life-partners. Possible good husband and wife. The longest journey begins with one step.

By the time their breakfast ended, they said they thought they were falling in love. They admired and complimented each other for what they had accomplished. They liked looking at each other, even if they were pretty high from the club liquor. They held hands during the final cup of coffee. He placed his arm around her shoulders as they left the Breakfast Inn. She put an arm around his waist. They ran through the drizzle to his glistening red car. Smiling through the moist air, he gently helped her inside.

They didn't want to part, to be alone again.

Smiling coquettishly, Tashyah said, "I should have fixed you that last cup of coffee at my house. I make very good coffee; do you like French roast?"

Grateful, because he had been wondering which tack to use to extend the night with her, he smiled and answered, "It's not too late. I have no need to rush home, and I could use a good cup of French roast coffee."

They sped through the street, rushing, perhaps, into a meaningful relationship. Hopeful. A little desperate even. He pulled into her long driveway as he looked her house over. "Not bad at all. I could live here comfortably," he thought to himself.

Tashyah checked his face to see if he recognized her position in life through the look of her house, and the yellow Mercedes parked, nestled under overhanging trees, in front of the garage. She was satisfied.

With low, mellow, sexy jazz flowing throughout the house, she prepared the coffee. Then poured it, steaming, into her new, expensive Swedish-design coffee cups. Smiling intimately at him, she served it in front of the living room fireplace he had relit. They talked a moment, about nothing. Then they looked into each other's eyes, and, finally, kissed until the coffee was cold.

The fire crackled and glowed warmly. The rains still came.

Together, they decided since it was still raining, Greg might as well spend the night. "Oh, not for sex," she explained, "of course not."

"Oh, of course not!" Greg explained. "I respect you too much for that. You mean more than that," he declared.

His arms around her shoulders, he drew her close to him. Her arm around his waist, they moved slowly, kissingly, to her bedroom.

He used a second bathroom to prepare himself for her bed. She prepared herself, then got into her bed . . . and posed, not unalluringly. He joined her with a small rush; he was in his underwear with his thin legs showing.

After the proper interval, where he could seem to keep his word and respect and she could keep her respect, they settled down to sleep. With his warm hand under the cover on her hip, his legs touching hers, he asked, "One last kiss? Then we'll go to sleep."

She turned to him, sighing. "Now, Greg, we said . . ." Then he kissed her anyway, and she said, "Ohhhmmm." They kissed . . . and kissed . . . and kissed, as the rain pelted the roof and the windows. Atmosphere rife with warmth and togetherness. And love?

At last, she turned her body to him, and he took it mindlessly.

In the beginning their bodies moved slowly, then the pace quickened to the rhythm of the rain that poured from the sky. They were both desperate, but not for sex. They were reaching for something that had not had time to grow. And something more than a body: their humanness, a human warmth.

Their loving lasted a long time. He couldn't reach the place he was striving for, and she could not get all of what she was reaching for. It was good . . . sometimes, frantic other times.

A long time later, when they were through, they lay slightly gasping for breath. She hadn't been satisfied because it wasn't exactly what she needed. "All that for a short, quick orgasm," she thought to herself.

He thought he had worked much harder than the situation should have demanded. He didn't really need it, but at least he had had another orgasm. He fell asleep as the thought almost entered his mind, "What I need is something more, something deeper." But, at least, they weren't home alone.

He slept fitfully because he wanted to be in his own bed, not that of a stranger. She was still a stranger; lovemaking had not changed that fact.

She slept uneasily, because, after all, he was a stranger. And in the morning, oh, my, he would see her in such a mess, drinking and staying up all night! "Oh, well," she thought as she drifted off to sleep, "I'll wake up first."

Greg woke early and got up with as much jostling of the bed as if he were alone. He yawned, stretched, relieved gas, scratched, washed up, and dressed. He refused the offer of coffee from a rudely awakened, and thankful, Tashyah.

She shut the front door behind him after pressing her card, with her phone number, into his hands. He slipped it into his pocket, hit her on the hip, and left. She heard his automobile smoothly roar as he took a while to warm it. She frowned.

"Damn! All my neighbors are gonna know someone was here all night!" Then, she yawned and waved the thought of neighbors away. "Oh, well."

Tired, she showered, dressed, and left her house to begin her day. Driving to work, someone played an oldie, Dinah Washington, singing, "What good is love that no one shares? Today you're young. Too soon, you're old." She turned it off. She wanted her mind clear for work.

The week went by at the usual pace, but time is a little lighter when you are expecting something good to happen. Saturday morning, Tashyah opened her eyes slowly. She was groggy, still half-asleep, really. She slid her hand over to the other side of her bed and . . . naturally, it was empty. She had been dreaming. She sat up and looked at her empty room.

As she showered, she thought, "He'll call me later today. I hope he doesn't make a pain of himself!" As she had her coffee, she mused, "This could grow into something real and good. He was really fine. A male fox. I can't remember the sex, too high, but, I'm sure it was good. And I know, he'll come back for more. I hope he is not the kind who just comes without calling first. I couldn't stand that. I really hope he doesn't make a pain of himself."

At moments throughout the day, she put on certain clothes and situated herself in different areas of the house: kitchen, living room, office, and even the garden. Busy doing things in attractive poses. So when he "just happened" to stop by, he would see she was attractive and much, much more than just a sex object.

But he didn't call and he didn't happen to drop by.

Sunday, instead of going to church "because he might have been busy yesterday and might drop by today," she lit the fireplace and sat in front of it. She gazed through her windows at her driveway that had no red Mercedes in it, only her yellow Mercedes that she seldom, if ever, put in the garage.

Her thoughts were, "A game player! Well, all right, I know that game, too!" She said that for the next several days when he didn't call. She didn't know his phone number, and he didn't call the next week either. She could look his number up, but her ego wouldn't allow that.

By the next busy holiday time, when The Club or some social happening was happening, Tashyah was planning to go out. Early in the evening, she relaxed in her lounge chair, gazing to the end of her foliage-full, lush backyard. Greg never had called; she tried to remember his face, but couldn't. "It was so dark in the club, and we drank so much. I remember the look in his eyes, but I can't get the feeling back of when he looked at me. But, I think of him all the time."

She laughed sadly, softly, at herself. "Him and a few others." She looked up to the skies, wondering where the sun had gone. Everything in her mind was dark. "But," she asked herself, "why should my life be dark? I have everything I need."

She laid her head back, thinking, "Why am I feeling so depressed? I'm too alone ... that's why. I feel like crying sometimes, and I don't know why I should. Someone will call one day, I know it. Somebody will! I can take the days, I'm busy then, Lord, but, oh, the nights, when there is no one caring about me, but me."

After a long interval, she raised her head, and gave herself the reasons men should pursue her. "I'm successful. Too good a catch to just pass by. I am somebody!"

She laid her head back again. Tears seeped beneath her eyelids and slid down the makeup on her face. She opened her eyes, and appealed to God, whom she very seldom spoke to, unless she was in some pain.

"Oh, God. God. God. I am so lonely. I am so lonely, I could almost die. You made Eve for Adam. Make someone love me. When is someone going to love me? Love me and stay with me?"

Some voice, she had almost pushed too far back to hear, said, "Try God."

But she shook that off, and then, really cried from her soul, into her life.

Meanwhile, across the brilliantly lighted city, was Greg. Greg was sitting on his couch in one of his smoking jackets, with the ascot from England he loved. His couch was situated in front of a huge mirror, in which he could see himself.

His phone was not ringing either. He had flicked through his address book, but was bored by all he found there.

Greg seldom mentioned "God." He always thought, "It's just a word anyway."

But, this evening, he was doing some new thinking. And so he thought, "God, why did you make this world so dead? So boring? I am too much man to be as lonely as I am. Where is Somebody?"

He couldn't remember Tashyah, or her body either.

He sat there trying to decide to call a buddy to go out somewhere and find somebody, women, who would, at least, be what he wanted, needed. Instead, he called God. "What the hell am I, ME, doing here wondering what to do with myself, and who to do it with?" He sighed. "Am I paying for something, God? Something I don't know anything about? Cause if I knew it, and it would make me happier, I would do it! Damn! I'm tired of this, this . . . loneliness! I got women who want me!" Then he smiled at himself. "You know I'm going crazy, cause here I am talking to You. I must be getting old! But, God, if You really are there, please send me the type of woman You know I need. Please! Because this being alone, ain't shit sometimes. I am a successful man, smart. But, God, I'm a lonely man."

He heard his aunt's little voice in his mind: "When Love finds you worthy, Gregory, it will be yours."

Annoyed, he shook her voice off and lifted his eyes to his mirror and contemplated his handsome face.

And now, let's you and I leave this city alone. Together.

Or is this your city?

Rushing Nowhere

I'm not sure why I want to tell you this story, because it isn't happy. But it was important to me. It's about coveting and jealousy. But there is something else to it, too. Life.

I am fourteen years old, and I was in love with my best friend's brother, Jamal. Whenever he was around my heart would pound so hard, and I could hardly breathe. I don't know if I still love him, but, oh, I did, I did!

Once he pinched the nipple of my breast as he smiled at me, and said, "I'm going to wait for you to grow up, cause you gonna be a beautiful woman someday!" I could hardly wait to get grown.

At Twyla's house, I stayed in his face; I wanted him to say something else to me, but he was always rushing somewhere. Being best friend to his sister, Twyla, gave me a close look at everything about him.

Jamal Pistle was thirty years old, and just about the handsomest man you ever want to meet! Somewhere between cute and pretty, but a masculine man. His personality was engagingly attractive, sparkling with wit and nonsense, romance, and jive.

All the women sought him out and he often answered their calls, because he loved hisself so much it spilled over and some of it fell on them. Not each one, but every one. He loved the female sex. He smiled at all of em.

He had a main lady, Kamika (who I hated), but he had a dozen stashes or extras. Since he was so fine, no matter what he did, she remained faithful. Still, even with Kamika on his arm, he just couldn't help turning his handsome head to see the one passing by. Someone who he didn't have on his arm, or in his big king-size bed . . . yet. I had seen that big bed and rubbed my hand across it.

His life was full. You hear me?

He was employed in a very good position, and made very good money. He loved clothes, and had quite a few, of excellent taste, they say. He was well-groomed. Regular appointments at the barber's. Always had a manicure, and sometime a pedicure. I ain't never had a pedicure, myself. My cousin gave me my manicure.

He didn't shop much in department stores, chile. He had his own tailor. A good one. Much of his money went out that way. I heard him say, "Hell, I'm young and healthy! I want everything I need to have a good, full life; and I am going to have one!" And he did.

Jamal didn't ever feel the years rushing slowly forward with him as he got older. Years do rush slowly; today you are twenty, and seems like next week you are fifty. I hear older ladies say that.

Jamal liked everything but his neighbors. Because they were always trying to tell him about the "hereafter" and God. And about going somewhere after death. Telling him to change his life, or he would be left behind. Dead forever.

They bored him, but they been knowing him since he was a young kid, I guess. A long time anyway. He avoided them. Then they wouldn't press on him, just smiled and waved out from their quiet, satisfied life.

"Left behind!" he would smirk, as he sauntered to his flashy riding car in his new finery. "Hell," he said again, "I'm in my prime! Young and strong. I spend too much on my clothes to let them sit in some church!"

And so he was, and so he lived his life. And so he should have, because it was his life and his choice. Can you hear me?

A few years passed as I got older. Jamal began to get bored with dancing and dining, parties and plays. Staying up till all kinds of hours. And women? He had already slept with most of them anyway. He still had his old neighbors, and their young daughter, Esther, a little older than I was, was growing up to be a beautiful young lady too. I didn't like her either.

When he could catch her in the yard or at the local market, he tried to talk to her. The thought of his neighbor's daughter excited him. Was a challenge to him, because they had tried to tell him, or implied, he was a no-good man; he wasn't good enough for them. She was so proper and always talking God-talk. "What had they said God's name was?" He laughed when he tried to remember and couldn't.

He thought to himself, "I might marry her. I know she is clean. And might be, probably is, a virgin. Ain't never had a virgin. I don't b'lieve anybody has touched that!" He frowned. "Them bitches I had wasn't near-bout no virgins."

He seemed to have forgotten Kamika, who was still waiting patiently for the times he took her out. She worked a poor little uneducated job, because she thought he was going to take care of her. She should have been in some college learning something to better her own condition so she could take care of herself. Wait a minute, I'm going to tell you why I say that.

I stopped being jealous of Kamika and got jealous of Esther. Actually, half the time I didn't know who to be jealous of there were so many.

The years had passed as Kamika was waiting to get married. They had been "engaged" bout five years. I think she was a fool, myself. Her life was like some fruit sittin on some vine: gonna fall off and hit that ground hard, squash or rot. Waiting for him.

I don't believe in long engagements, myself. If you love me, marry me. If you going to do something, do it. I know you hear me.

So, he was thinking of Esther. But that young lady always smiled pleasantly, and kept moving on her way. Sometimes she said, "Don't be left out, Jamal." He would laugh a little with her as she moved down some aisle in a store. He would watch her as she walked away from him. Smirking, he would return to his own shopping needs. "Left out! I never have been 'left out.'"

Some time later, six months or so, Jamal was out on some wonderful occassion, having "a natural ball," as he would say. His lady of the night, that night, was his faithful Kamika. Both dressed to the sixes (as he would say), in the very best. Sparkling, flashing, in the crowded party. Cocktails in hand, everyone greeted them. They knew Jamal well.

A few of his other ladies were there, flashing angry looks from the corners of their eyes at Kamika and, later, alluring eyes at Jamal; whining whispers from some, angry whispers from others as they had quick occasions. Just as quickly, Jamal flashed back, "Call you later." Women were his power, so long as they wanted him. Everyone had a ball. It was the greatest party of the year. Everyone said so!

Jamal led Kamika to his car and, though a little tipsy, gallantly opened the door for her. She stepped into the smell of leather and plush seating, gently. I know cause I've seen her do it.

She had not had as much to drink as Jamal. He had wanted to drive off like a blade of light in his flashy sports car, before everyone got away so he could leave a scene behind him; like riding away on his beautiful horsepower with the beautiful damsel. And he did. Everyone talked about it later. "How handsome! How sharp! How cool! That car!" The car was part of his power, as long as he could pay for it.

They were going to drive to Kamika's apartment (couldn't go to his; telephone too busy). They smiled at each other as they talked about the party. Kamika wanted to talk about marriage while Jamal was in such a good mood. She had decided to take her life back to school, get a degree, and meet some new men. She thought, "If he's not going to marry me now, I'm not going to wait anymore. I might as well do better things with my time!"

But all he could talk about was, "Such food! Oh, the clothes! Did you see that outfit Earl had on? Screamin! And all that liquor! That good music." He laughed happily. "It was just a good party! That's all there is to it!"

As he was thinking of whom he would call first, to get his private business back in control, he reached across the seat for her hand. Said, "And I took my baby! My baby! You know I love you, baby!" He thought control was another power of his; he could think of more than one woman at a time.

Jamal always drove carefully. Careful to see who was seeing him, and who he could see. He liked to cruise, and this night his liquor told him to drive home on one of the well-lit boulevards, still busy, and full of people. I know cause I've seen him do it. He wanted his car to be seen. He wasn't drunk. But someone else was.

At some place in a fairly busy strip of street, Jamal was, impatiently, waiting for a chance to go around a truck. Another driver swerved out, from nowhere it seemed, at an enormous speed, and headed straight into Jamal's flashy fine automobile, one of Jamal's main powers. And, you know these new cars are practically made of plastic. The other car seemed to rage as it tore right into the rear of Jamal's power automobile with great speed. It hit, smashing, bending and tearing as it crashed, and crushed both people and fine car into the truck, crushing both Jamal and Kamika. To death, chile.

Everyone talked about it. "Too terrible!"

Kamika's pitiful family took their daughter, sister, niece, grandchild, to the funeral home and gave her an honorable, beautiful, flower-filled, closed-casket funeral. Her family and friends grieved. "Poor beautiful, young Kamika never even had a chance to marry or have children of her own. She just gone. Gone." Or, "I told her bout that bastard! He took up her life while she was alive; now he done took her life all the way to the end. She dead now, can't do nothin else no more."

I went to her funeral because I really felt bad for her. I didn't hate her anymore. I liked her.

The memorial for Jamal was filled with people who brought food and much liquor. They played the latest music and had a ball! A regular ball! He would have loved it. Everyone talked about it.

And they talked about Jamal. "How terrible! He wasn't even old; somewhere in his thirties, I think. And that beautiful car. Destroyed! Just crushed to dea . . . pieces!"

"How terrible!"

"How sad. Such a waste."

Everyone talked about it.

His women were there, of course. As they checked the crowd out for their next man, they said, "And so handsome! He was fine, fine, fine, and could screw you to death, real good!" I was surprised when I heard the woman say that because she was one of the real ugly ones! He really didn't miss anyone.

A few people came to the closed-casket funeral the next day. Most of his friends were too hung-over from the memorial wake.

"There will be so many people there they won't miss me. Won't even notice I wasn't there," as they took two aspirin, turned over, and went back to sleep.

Then . . . they forgot him. As people do.

After a few days, "everyone" didn't talk about him.

I don't know if God remembered him, because Jamal had never introduced himself to God. Jamal probably wouldn't care, because he didn't believe in God anyway. Jamal would just have to wait until Judgment Day, unless you were already judged on the day you died. But, who knows?

Jamal lay in his coffin, looking as best the funeral director could manage, six feet under the surface of the earth. Just left behind when all his friends went home.

Poor Kamika. She waited too long, but the waiting is over, she is resting in peace.

Poor Jamal, always rushing, at last going nowhere. Ashes to ashes and dust to dust. Left behind.

Now, you may think this is a too sad story. But the reason I'm telling you is I used to be jealous of Jamal and Kamika. And now . . . I can't hardly tell you how I feel. I feel sad for them. And I'm almost ashamed to be happy for me. But what can I say? I am happy for me that I didn't grow up in time for him to rush me going nowhere.

I'll be in college soon. There are plenty of young men there, and a education for me too! I'm rushing for that. Going to take myself somewhere!

Just-Life Politics

You know, when you talk about somethin you need to know what you are talkin about. And I do! I know what I'm talkin bout cause I'm talkin bout myself and what happened to me.

I do domestic work; been doin it all my life, since I was thirteen years old, and I am forty-three years old now. Been workin on the same job too. Of course, you got to be someplace if you on this earth livin and my place to be was on my job at work.

I ain't shamed of bein a domestic; I raised four children and two of em went to college. So there.

Now, that might not seem important, and it probly ain't to you, but I always been a body to try to understand the people around me. I been workin thirty years for the Bsurds, who own the house I work in. He is a politician and she just stays home doin whatever she feels like. (Findin somethin for me to do, usually.) The pay was almost fair, wasn't too much, but it was better than nothin. And some poor women get even less than I do.

Howsomever all that may be, my points was I never was a "political" woman. I didn't know nothin real deep but the Bible, and I wasn't never gonna mean nothin to almost nobody, so I just worked and left all them politics to smarter people. I learned what I learned from the folks I worked for. They said they was conservatives. Conservative everything. They hated and talked about people who they called liberals like they was fools and dogs.

I looked them words up in their dictionary that sits in their own house. So they sure did have a chance to look things up and know what they mean. But Mr. Bsurd must not have looked them words up, or we just don't agree on em. But they done changed it around so they done made "liberal" kind of a bad word.

Now, I believe in savin money, but I believe in helpin people, when I can, too!

Mr. Bsurd is a mighty rich man. Mighty rich! And Mrs. Bsurd was already rich when he married her years ago; her family had money. But do you know I started out workin, by the hour, for one dollar and fifty cents a hour. It took me ten years to get to two dollars a hour. Thirty years and now I'm up to four dollars and fifty cents a hour. They hate to hit that five-dollar mark. He say conservative is to help people learn to save their money, and he is helpin me learn that. My mama already taught me that. Good thing she did.

And he got meat in their pots and on their table every day for years. I cooked every meal they ate. I sure would have liked meat on my table for my children when they was growin up, at least once a week.

Mr. Bsurd votes in one of them Houses in Washington, D.C. Been doin it for some time now. Both of his grown children went to grand colleges; they sit in high places now, because of their learnin, I 'magin. But one of his votes closed all the libraries round where I live. I was glad they was there cause my kids used them for studyin work. But they're closed now.

Another thing he thought was that free clinics and free things was making it possible for people to get off from what everybody else has to pay. He didn't think that was fair to some who had the money to pay. Them clinics almost all closed now. He thinks he did a good job. I'll tell you this, there was times when if that free clinic-hospital wasn't there, my family would'a died and that would'a killed me.

I hear him talkin to his dinner friends, saying, "All these people don't need no education. What they gonna do with it? We need to close these schools that serve the community that ain't gonna raise nothin but dope addicts and prostitutes anyway!" I heard em! They got a plan! You betta watch out little children, all colors!

I know some of what he thinks because he talks to me sometime about politics when I'm servin him breakfast or somethin when he have to eat alone and ain't nobody but me to talk to. He loves to talk. Talk and smile. When television came out, I would see him on it, talkin and smilin. Talkin bout lovin God and helpin "the people." Ain't I a people? He want me to vote for him, but he don't vote for me. They always talkin bout cuttin somethin for the poor and sick. All they cut for themself is taxes.

Anyway, I have worked for him from his marriage to his old age. I done heard him, with his mouth full of Jesus, tearing "liberal" people and thoughts down, and I know he lied sometimes. Cause people starving all over this world, and I b'lieve they pays people, farmers, not to grow food. Now, that ain't like Jesus at all.

God ain't made this big earth and put all these people on it without there being enough to feed em. But when some people have money and is full of food, they don't mind other people bein hungry. In fact, on TV they say, "Everything is goin long just fine!"

Anyway, howsomever all that is, this is what I want to tell you.

That man, my boss, Mr. Bsurd, not too long ago he got sick. After a few years of taking medicine, going to his doctor, struggling to keep his place in Washington, D.C., he had to retire. He was only in his late fifties, I guess.

Doctors and hospitals is high costs! He fussed and fought about it . . . and he had money! He was always grumbling over how they treat him and he had held some positions in politics! He would tell em that, but it didn't help as much as he wanted.

He started goin to church more, though; him and his little wife. He prayed to get well. The whole church prayed for him. He asked me to pray for him one day when I took a tray to his room. I told him, "You got to pray for yourself, Mr. Bsurd. I'd be glad to pray for you but it takes all my time up just praying for myself and my family and some poor friends I got who are suffering." See, I got friends, black and white and brown, old and young, who are poor and struggling to survive.

He looked at me out of his sad face and asked, "Don't you believe in God, Elanora?"

I looked back at him out of my sad face. "Of course I b'lieve in God, you know that, Mr. Bsurd. I just got so many friends that is poor, out of work, and sick that I need to use my prayers for them. But you always talk about God, so I know you must be close to Him, and when you ask Him for somethin He sure is goin to help you. You don't need my poor little pitiful prayers." As I left his room, he looked at me like he was thinkin bout somethin important.

I wasn't tryin to be mean or nothin. The truth is the light. And that's what I told him. After that, he seemed to wait for me to come in there, so he could ask me again.

Finally, the time came when he knew his time was running out. He was going to die.

Ohhhhh, he prayed. He prayed and had everybody who came to see him get on their knees and pray with him. Even me; I gave in; I wouldn't get on my knees (I'm too old and I got to clean his house) but I prayed over him. I wasn't nothin special so I don't know if God even listened to me. I knew some of the people who got down on their knees to pray with him though, and I KNEW God didn't hear them; they was too far away from Him. Take me at my word! Cause I been around here a long time and I know em!

One day he asked me to have my church to pray over him.

Now, he ain't never cared bout me or my church or anybody starvin to death in it or needin a job, before. Took me thirty years to get a three-dollar raise and he knew I was tryin to raise three children at that time. I stayed workin for him because I needed that steady work to send them to school and college. Now, I'm old, and my children help me. But I don't want to be too big a burden on them, cause life takes all you got to give now. All life don't take from you, the tax man comes sneakin up on you with new laws to take the rest of whatever you got left.

Anyway, what I want to tell you . . . I was so surprised I could'a fell out! I wish I could speak better words.

Mr. Bsurd was a very sick man, sad, scared, and sick. So, this time, I got down on my tired, sore knees, like he asked me to, and I prayed with him. When we was gettin through, and I was gettin up (breathing heavy from all that effort cause I'm a heavy-built woman), he grabbed my hand and looked up at me with them scared eyes, said, "Elanora? What do you know about God? I mean . . . do you think God will forgive me any . . . mistakes . . . I may have made?"

I'm a little shamed of myself, but I didn't really mean him any mental harm. I asked him, "Well, it depends on the way God thinks, Mr. Bsurd. Do you think God is a liberal or a conservative?"

He looked into my eyes for a minute then moved his eyeballs slowly to look through his huge window at the sky. He didn't say anything else so I began gathering what I was going to take back downstairs.

I almost jumped at his voice cause I didn't expect to hear him speak again, I thought he was thinking. He said, "From now on, when you pray, pray for God to be a liberal. I don't want to die. I don't want Him to be conservative with His blessings. Pray that Jesus be a liberal."

I smiled when I answered him, "Jesus was a liberal. And he didn't fool with no politics. If they had votin when he was alive, he didn't vote. He said his Father's kingdom was the only good, fair, just, and merciful one. And not to put our faith in mankind, because mankind was corrupt. If you catch a good person, cherish them as if they was a treasure, for they are few. And I b'lieve that. Jesus just loved people, even if they didn't love his Father, but he loved them more if they did love his Father."

Slowly, tears began to roll down Mr. Bsurd's face. He was crying. I felt so sorry for him. But I had to remember you must reap what you sow. Maybe the glitter of the world had blinded him, so he didn't know what he had been sowing while he was sowing. But the Bible is a best-seller book. Ain't no way you can't know. There was one in this house of his, seldom if ever used.

As I went down the stairs, back to the kitchen, I was thinking of him, Mr. Bsurd. This man had hated liberals all his life. He was one of those who helped make it a "bad" word. Now he wanted Jesus and God to be liberals. For his sake! But Jesus and God been done been their own way since forever.

Well, all I can say, for myself, is you live and sometimes you learn. Sometimes life don't get real to you . . . till it's bout to go away. Then, it's too late. The end done got to you before the reality could set in.

But I ain't the final judge. I don't know nothin bout no politics no way. I just know the politics of plain ole life. I know what happened to me and, kind'a to just about all poor people everywhere.

Well, life is life. Here I am standin up here tellin you all my business when I got work to do. You go on long now. I got to get on bout my business.

I got to keep my job. It's all I got!

I got to get on back to work, chile.

Oysters and Pearls

Latesha was a lovely twenty-year-old girl-woman. Hazel eyes complimented the rich chestnut of her shoulder-length, luxurious hair. She had full breasts that were her own, a small waist, and hips that were ready for childbearing or a wonderful cradle for other hips to lie upon. Her pretty hands were slender with nails she kept manicured to match her small, perfect toes. Such gifts life gave her at birth. She was some kinda woman.

She often said, "I didn't go to school pass the seventh grade. But, that's all right. I was born with everything I need, to do whatever I want to do!" And she was almost right! But, she hadn't gone to school long enough to learn all the things there were to do.

And nobody told her.

Inside her mind and body, often filled with the semen of a few strange men, and a friend or two, was a sad swirling of pain and misery she kept covered with small dreams, beautiful clothes, and lately, liquor. But, everybody, men and women, desired her. They wanted to reach out to beauty, paw and cling to it, tear and waste it in their hands. But the only reward for that is the prelude; they make you feel like you are a star come down from the heavens.

"Hell," she would say, "I got a good man. You seen that big, long car he drives! And his diamonds and gold shine enough to light up this whole street! What b'longs to him, b'longs to me." She would throw her pretty head back, and laugh. "The world is my oyster!"

A laughing, jealous woman-friend might say, "Yeah, but every oyster ain't got a pearl. What you got of your own?"

Latesha had the quick answer. "I'ma get me some pearls! Hell, I got me! Don't need nothing else!" Everyone would laugh, as if at a good joke.

No one told her.

Latesha had come up the hard way. But, there are more than a million ways to come up the hard way, and more than a million ways to make it turn out right.

But, nobody told her.

Latesha loved the tinsel-sparkle of the night life. She met many people, men in night life, who were there to partake of what life seemed to be. . . . All these men had learned, or thought, was of any value was a great car, a few diamonds, and some shining gold to catch a woman with. Women made money, so a man wouldn't have to have any other skills. Anyone can gamble, but not anyone can win on a regular basis. So. A woman's stock in trade never seemed to run out. Her body was his best bet.

Somebody didn't tell him either. Or he didn't listen.

Latesha thought she loved the man she had; but she really loved the smell and sight of what seemed like success. (He would be in prison in three more years.)

She had girlfriends who no one had told either.

They all loved the "good life," laughing and carefree. They stole the very best clothes, wore sparkling rhinestones until they could get a real diamond, which would usually be taken and pawned by their lovin man. They dreamed of big things, like catching a rap star with all their flashing money. They hung around the places the star athletes patronized. Hoping . . . Dreaming . . . Waiting.

No one told them.

Latesha turned a few tricks, slyly, quietly, so she would have money to flash and spend. Her man didn't give her any; that was against his philosophy. Part of the popular philosophy, among her friends, was that only fools worked.

One night she met a wonderful man who was spending money like it was rock pebbles. His eyes were on her. So were her man's eyes. The man spent her way along the bars until, away from her man, he drew her close to him. He spoke into her ear, fast and warm. She laughed, and she thought.

Over the next few days she saw him several times, until they became friends. Then he whispered deeper into her ear. He said sweet things, fly things, cool things, as he was supposed to. He said them well because he had a lot of practice; they were the same things he always said over and over because they were the things women want to hear. "Some women fall in love just from listening," he told his friends.

No one told him there are different kinds of women. But, then, he was probably only going to meet the kind that he could impress. Maybe. And, after all, what did he really have to offer love?

No one could tell him anything, anymore.

It came to pass that he arranged an assignation with Latesha. For a little money, of course. No matter how much money it is, it's always just a little. Can you really put a price on it? No one could ever prove a price to me.

In this man's body there was rushing through his veins a crooked-shaped, mean, ugly germ that meant serious business. He was that kind of man, who, even after certain signs from his body, thought he was invincible. So he didn't go to a doctor who might have helped him. I guess that's what they mean when they say you can't judge a book by its cover, cause he looked good.

Somehow, he hadn't heard anyone when they were talking about things like this.

Latesha and the quick-money man made mad, passionate love all day, two or three times, in a very luxurious room. You had to really "dress" before you went to that hotel.

Each time she went to the bathroom she grinned, and gloried in all the bright lights beaming on her. She looked even more beautiful, framed by the velvety wallpaper, the marble floors and walls. She smiled at herself as she flicked out the light to go back to the money-man for some more of his loving.

The germ, and all its relatives, was sleeping in the warmth of the blood flowing, with passion, through the money-man's veins. Soon they would awaken to fly through any opening to the warmth of Latesha. Once there, the germs looked around and saw all the fresh, new flesh to devour. They would begin a party of their own, with their hungry relatives. The germs did not need, or even know about, a mirror; they have no cares or feelings except the capacity to grow . . . and keep growing. In fact, the germs would not like to be looked at.

No one had to tell them what to do, they were born knowing.

Latesha left the money-man with her pockets full and her uterus full. She went to her really nice apartment and cleaned herself up. But the ugly, little mean germs just shook their heads "no, no" and didn't go anywhere. Satisfied, because they were already going through Latesha's veins.

Latesha looked into her mirror, smiled, and said, "I told you the world is my oyster! This is some big-time money, for nothing I'm going to miss!"

No one could tell her. And she hadn't listened when she was told.

When next Latesha rode in her man's pretty, long car, they stopped to eat dinner at a really grand place because this assured them they were really grand people. Then, he took her home, to her apartment, to bed.

Well, who could tell him? He hadn't listened, in his youth, when they did tell him.

A perfectly lovely lifetime dwindled away a little more every day. Passing without notice amid the arrogance and ignorances of youth.

Her lovely genes started getting together with her man's genes and formed a little human heart. She was not unhappy, because she thought she loved him. She told her man the happy news. He looked at her as though she was crazy.

You see, he knew, now, about the busy germ. He didn't know who had given him that mean, ugly germ, but had definitely thought of her. You see, he was *her* man, but she was not *his* woman. Several times, he had decided to ease her out of his pretty automobile and life. "But the woman's body is just so delectable! At least," he thought, "it was, but now it's getting plump and thick." His heart was changing its mind. He never minded changing his mind.

He asked her, "Have you told the daddy?"

"You are the daddy, darlin."

"Get serious, Latesha."

"Well"—she was confused—"I am serious."

"Not if you say I'm the daddy. That ain't my baby. What I look like with a baby, bein a daddy!? You done lost your mind! And get out my car anyway, I got to be somewhere."

Nobody had told her?

Those beautiful eyes of Latesha's wept as she cried her heart out. She prayed to God, whom she hadn't given a thought to during all this time. She prayed to the stars and the moon. But, of course, they didn't answer.

The nurse told her it may be too late for an abortion. She also told Latesha that she had a million ugly, mean germs going around through her lovely young body. Germs that meant Latesha and the baby no good at all.

With no real money (the money-man was in some other city now, or some other woman), she went home to the small crowded apartment of her mother.

The same mother who had tried to warn Latesha when she dropped out of school. The mother who had tried to tell Latesha about several important things. The mother Latesha had shook her hips at, and told, "It's my body, and my life! And I'm grown! I can do whatever I want to with my body! It ain't none of your business what I do!"

So, someone did try to tell her.

The mother, already one of the working poor, took Latesha in, begrudgingly. Well, she couldn't afford the two other children she was raising, and had to support and care for. She had tried to tell Latesha. And she had her own struggle with her own life; everybody is in pursuit of happiness. In search of satisfaction. It sure is a struggle.

Nobody had told the mother either. Maybe.

Somewhere along that line, the baby came. Ohhh, what a world it entered. No one wanted her.

Latesha had no job, had no skills, had no baby-sitter, had no money, had no place of her own. Had nothing. She began to turn tricks, in earnest, out there with her old, what? Friends? Eventually, she moved in with an old, stingy, dirty ole man. "Just for a while," she said, "till I get on my feet." He wouldn't let her bring the baby, so she sneaked off one day, leaving the baby on her mother's bed.

One day, the county took the baby, that beautiful, sick baby, and put her in a foster home. She was a sweet baby, as cute as could be. Her mother, who the child was born to look to for protection, had set the baby's life, her future. If she lived, maybe someday someone would tell this baby. But, would she hear?

Latesha is somewhere now, trying to live a life. Trying to get back to where she thought she was. She was.

She knows more now. But bitterness is woven throughout her brain, filling the holes in her little wisdom. Her smile is not as bright. She is not as lovely or beautiful. As they say, the song has ended, but the melody lingers on. Faintly.

She has a real bad case of the bottom-blues. She has met so many flashy men who only want the money she makes with her body. The people she is around, can't tell her what they don't know. They need help their own selves.

Truth be told, she ain't got time. They never did kill that germ.

She used to always speak about the world being her oyster; she never thought about the pearls of wisdom. But, she never speaks of oysters anymore, anyway. And real pearls seem to be out of reach.

Wait a Minute, World!

I *was a quiet* little girl. I had a little rocking chair and was always rocking and watching those around me through my eight-year-old eyes. Wasn't looking for anything special because I didn't know anything special to watch for. I didn't know anything much about life, but I knew there must be something to it, or in it, because people were so busy doing something all the time.

People were still new to me, almost everything they did seemed to be interesting if only for a short while.

I had a brother so I played a lot of boy games with him. He played hard, so I knew how to fight and wrestle a little. I could also throw a football, not real good but I could hold and throw it right. But my favorite thing was dreaming, reading, and watching people.

My daddy didn't like to work for other people, white people. He was from the South. He had worked on a car lot there, and one day his boss asked him to take and park a car. He drove to California where he had a married sister who had been urging him to come there. That's how I came to be born in California.

He repaired cars in our huge backyard. He separated metals making piles, one from the other, and took them to a metal junk-yard to sell. I never do remember him being broke.

We always had plenty food to eat, because he loved food. My mama did too, and she could really cook. We had a big ole round wood table in the kitchen and everybody sat at every meal. You had to eat when everybody else did just to be sure you got some food.

Anyway, that was a piece of how I grew up.

We had two neighbors I watched. In Berkeley, a long time ago, you could live anywhere you had the money to buy. We didn't live in the best neighborhood and we didn't live in any poor neighborhood. I don't remember any ghettos of poor people. Everybody was kind'a poor because a depression was going on or going out. I don't remember which one, cause we had enough. But I know we got vaccinations and shots free from the city at a clinic on University Avenue. Everybody went, I guess.

But what I was telling you was about our neighbors. On one side was an old, old (it seemed to me) Spanish man who lived in a great big two-story house, all alone. He must'a had some money because he took care of that house, but he drank a lot. He was quiet and kept to hisself.

He was friends with my father, but everybody liked my father because he was friendly and generous to everybody. He even brought people home to feed them. They didn't know it at first, but he was going to put them to work cleaning his garage or separating metal or something. But they were going to have to work; no laying around at our house, cause my daddy worked all the time.

One man, Dave (I don't remember his last name, if I ever knew it), was a good worker and stayed with us kind'a a long time. My mama said he could even have dinner at our round table if he was sober. My daddy paid him a little money and gave him the small room off the garage. Dave made it neat. Dave had a drinking problem too.

Our neighbor on the other side was white. I don't know what kind of "white" they were, Irish, English, German, or what. I just knew they were white and nice. A real nice pretty redheaded young woman with a husband and two children. A nice family. They were friendly, but were busy so kept to themselves and their business. Both grown-ups worked. Nobody partied together. In a depression there ain't nothing to party about.

I just lived, grew, watched, and learned about life and people. Didn't know what I was learning all the time, but it was life and I was very interested in life. I still am.

My best friend was my yellow dog, Lady, and a tree. They were who I talked to and played with. And my mama, of course. I could talk to and ask my mother anything, and I did. She always had an answer.

I didn't play with other kids very much. They had a messy way of living: fighting, arguing, doing little nasty things to each other. Their noses running, mine too. Clothes poor and most times dirty, mine too. But I liked being alone watching them make each other happy at play for a while, then watching them fight for a while. Seemed silly to me, so I would go off with my dog or go sit by my tree. I'd be alone and think, or play secretary all by myself. In peace.

Then . . . this day came along that I'm going to tell you about.

The white lady next door asked my mother if my father could take her across town to pick up her sister; she had had a call that her sister was ill and needed someplace to get well. She wanted to go get her sister, pick her up, and bring her home. My mama said yes, so my daddy said yes too.

I rode with my father and our neighbor. It was night and I remember sitting in the car waiting. A bright light was shining on the porch of the house. Daddy helped our neighbor bring her sister out to the car.

I remember the sister was slender, very pretty, and redheaded. Beautiful golden red hair. I wished my hair was golden red like that. I've always been in awe of shining beauty; nature or people.

I stared at the pretty lady. I had thought she would be sick, but she was drunk. I was glad because I rather her be drunk than really sick because you can get sober. And she was not ugly, nasty drunk. She was sad drunk.

When we got home my daddy helped our neighbor take her sister into her house. In the darkness of the car, I watched to the very end of their door closing. I cried for her sadness even though I didn't know what real sadness was, I could feel what it was. Then my father parked in our driveway and we went in our house.

Now there was more I didn't understand about life. I couldn't understand why such a pretty woman would be so sad and would want to be so drunk. I didn't know what alcoholism was or what poverty could do. There was always some liquor at our house, but nobody drank it much. My mama did sometimes. Then she would dance if somebody played our piano or a record. That sounds like we had something, but we didn't really.

Anyway, I heard our neighbor tell my daddy she had gotten her sister and they were going to keep her away from liquor and sober until she could get on her feet.

Then I forgot about it because something else probably took over my mind. I read a lot of books. My mother was always reading every chance she got between whatever housework, whippings, and cooking she did. Sometimes she put on her overalls and went out to help Daddy separate the metals. But, mostly, we would sit up on the bed and both be reading. I learned to love books. Thank God!

I don't know how much time passed; maybe a week, maybe a day, maybe a month, but it wasn't a year. But one day when I was out playing in the backyard I looked up and saw the next-door sister come walking down our driveway toward my father. She had long pretty legs with the wind whipping her dress around her knees, and that golden hair was shining in the sun, and blowing in the wind.

She asked my father to take her back, while her sister was at work, to the house where he had picked her up. She was home alone. Daddy's eyes got big and round as he stared at her, seriously. I saw that and I remember because Daddy was usually playing funny things with us kids. I thought he was playing with her. I knew my daddy knew what our neighbor wanted for her sister. Anyway he laughed as he told her he couldn't do it right then, he had a few other things he had to do.

My father weighed about two hundred pounds and loved to laugh, so she didn't get mad at him. He was pleasant in his refusal. She stayed around talking to him and Dave. I guess she was lonely. I stayed around because I was looking at life.

Pretty soon my daddy did have to go off to pick up something for his garage. He went in the truck. He told the lady she should go home. But he left Dave and the lady alone. I think about that sometimes, now that I am older. Because I love my dad, but I thought something was wrong. Dave was sober while he worked, but Dave was a drunk.

After my dad drove off, Dave laughed and talked with the lady a little while. Then he went into our house and came back out with a bottle of wine. I was just a child, but I knew he shouldn't drink in front of that lady.

I was leaning on a car set up on blocks with no tires on it. I watched him when he took his bottle into his little room off the garage, and he was laughing. I was looking at her as she thought for only a quick minute; then she followed him into the room. His room. His door was open. I didn't move a muscle. I suspected something. I felt something in life was about to happen, but I didn't know exactly what.

Dave stuck his head around the door, I guess to see if I was still there; I was. He pushed that door shut. He closed my eyes, out.

I still don't think I was nosy. I was curious. No, I needed to know what life was going on in that room. The drama in my mind was almost unbearable. I tried every way I could to find a hole in those walls. I didn't try to sneak; I was serious. But I never did find one. I heard low laughter from both of them. Then, after a while, I didn't hear a thing. Nothing.

Then, my daddy was back. He drove down the driveway, parked and asked me where Dave was. I pointed to Dave's room without saying a word. That's when my daddy sent me into the house. I wasn't mad, but I felt cheated or something.

I don't know what happened with Dave and the lady, but I still felt sorry for her. I felt sorry for her sister who was trying to help her. I didn't feel the same exact way about Dave. I still felt sorry for Dave sometimes, but I had stopped liking him, didn't enjoy his little play jokes. I didn't like him to touch me, even playfully, anymore. Didn't thoroughly understand why. He was less to me. Maybe grown people do things like he did, but there was something cheap and crooked about it to me. He took advantage of her pain. She let him, but he kicked her when she was down. I was seven or eight years old and I knew it, why didn't he?

I didn't know exactly what happened till some years later when I was old enough to figure it all out. I know her sister was real hurt when she came home to find her sister drunk again. I know the lady was soon gone from her sister's house.

There is a sad failure between everybody. I'm a feeler kind of person. I feel most everything, even things from across the city or the world. Especially if they are sad or hurting someone. Don't know why but sometimes the whole damn world looked sad to me and I would cry for no reason I knew at all. Then and now, even since I'm grown.

As I think back and know what I know now, about the depression, poverty, hunger, sickness, homelessness, and hope, and all the things people have to deal with. Alcoholism was prevalent then and it's prevalent now. We've had plenty government, plenty more taxes, and they ain't fixed but a very few things for the people, and every time they get, or might get, a good government they lie him off the map. And the people let the liars keep lying.

Anyway, back to that day I was telling you about. I don't know the difference between Mexican and Spanish, so the neighbor on the other side of our house could have been either one. Like I told you, he took care of his house and was a quiet, older man. Grey hair and all.

The kids in our neighborhood never took notice of him until he came out to tell them to get off his garage or out of his yard or something. But there were days they were sure to notice his doings.

I believe his name was Gonzalez. He used to have a prostitute come to his house once a week or once a month, I can't remember. I don't know how we all knew that was what she was, but we knew. She was delivered or drove there in a pretty car every once in a while. She was always different, I think, and always dressed, looking really pretty as she tripped lightly over the cobblestones in his yard on the way to his front door.

The kids would stare at her, some of them would say "hello" as she passed by. We thought she must be a movie star. Well, kids can think two or three things about the same thing as they figure it out.

I watched, as usual, for a couple of times when those horrible kids waited for her to get inside and him to close the door. They gave him a few minutes to get in bed (they thought), then they would throw big rocks at his house. The rocks hit the wood with a big thud! Ten or fifteen rocks at a time. There were some horrible kids on our block! Then they would hurry around trying to find bigger rocks for bigger noises.

I waited for a window to break, but they aimed pretty good. It looked like they were having such fun that I finally rushed out to join them. Rocks were thrown until the lady came out, hastily, rushing to her car.

Mr. Gonzalez would come rushing behind her, drunk, waving his arms and cursing us. We had destroyed his moment of peace or joy.

It was fun, for a minute. It was fun until my feelings (I told you I'm a feeler) made me think about what we were doing to Mr. Gonzalez. I thought of that old tired-looking man that was friends with my father. He was trying to have company, a romantic moment maybe, in peace, his once a month, or once a week time for a little pleasure with a lady. And there we were out there ruining what little he had left of his life. What's the fun in that? I felt sorry for him and I stopped throwing rocks at his house.

It must have been the worst of times for everybody, like that writer Dickens said.

Now, what I told you happened in less than three months in my life growing up. Seven or eight years old. What must have happened around me, and everyone, that we didn't pay attention to?

I cried a lot growing up. People, even my mama, didn't always understand why I cried. But . . . something about life and some people made me feel so sad, like I could see something bad, something unhappy around them.

I haven't cried much like that for a long, long time. But I still feel the sadness around people. Or maybe it's just me. A silly kid at the time, a silly woman now. But, I remember, about that time my father's Japanese friends were forced to leave their houses they owned to go to some strange place because of the new war. My mother went to help them pack, and they were crying.

I saw all of them cry. Their kids, my friends, were red-eyed and sniffling as they helped their parents get ready to leave. They had to leave their house, their dad had to leave his job or business if they had one, their school, their friends. Their home, just think of that! So this was and is a sad, sad world most of the time. I bet someone is being forced to leave their families and homes right now.

My childhood always seemed happy to me. Well, it was; we

laughed a lot at my house. Then this memory slipped into my mind, right back into my feelings. With everything else happening in the world today, it was too sad for me, right now, to look into the reality of life and my childhood. I am just glad there is a God and He has a purpose and a plan!

My heart hurts for whoever in the world is hurting. I know many are. I scream out of the feelings in my soul and say, "Wait a minute, World! Wait a minute!"

And, for some reason, I wanted to tell somebody. So I told you.

The Party

This is not going to be no long story cause I do not like talking bout this stuff. It was just such a blockbuster, I can't help tellin it! My name ain't important cause you never gonna hear from me again, but my cousin's name is Lucilla. We call her "Lucy" for short.

It was early this summer and I was going to the city to visit my relatives. That was going to be my vacation. Well, working vacation. I started college, sociology major, two years ago and you know I needed a vacation. I'm also working at a city medical clinic, for a few credits while I am here. Still, I was hapPY! Glad to be gettin away from home. Cause I always have fun here with my cool cousins.

This is what I'm going to tell you. The Sunday it happened started on a brilliant, sun-filled morning. Perfect for going to church in the fine clothes you had selected on Friday or Saturday evening. Smiles, handshakes, light laughter, and the proper respect for the minister who beamed over all the people at his church. The few new, and the many old faithful.

The sermon gave everyone a bright, optimistic perspective for the day. Most of the people thought the minister had done his job well. They tried to prove it in the collection basket.

Several of the ladies and gentlemen were planning a full and busy day. A baby shower, a football game, a movie theatre among other things. Many of them knew they would meet each other later at the Come In nightclub to dance to a combo of musicians that could really get down with the beat. I danced so much I was totally exhausted.

But, I'm getting ahead of myself.

My cousin Lucy is a very attractive thirty-four-year-old woman. Single and looking for her next husband. She is not desperate, just wanted a man in her life. She thinks you are not complete without a man by your side.

Her friend Delores went to church with us. After church, she was just moving around the people, talking to her friends. Especially one new person, Delbert, and some friend of his, making plans for later that night. They didn't look too cool to me, kind'a like they might rip off the collection plate if they had a chance. But God s'posed to love everybody, so who am I to judge?

A lot of people were going to the club that night. They were from twenty to forty-five years or so, old. I wasn't interested in any of the men unless they could dance. I knew Wilcox, a friend of mine, was going to be there. That Wilcox sure can dance and never gets tired!

So the day began clean, innocent, and safe. Time passed swiftly; everyone had things to do for that day. A baby shower, a movie theatre, a football game, or a visit to see somebody sick. Throughout the day on the telephone and all, people kept talking about going to the dance club that night. The world was moving on its merry way! For good or evil. "No one can halt it," my mama says.

Well, to skip all the rest of the things that won't interest you, we got to the club about eleven o'clock. Two cars full of my cousins and friends. You could hear the horns and drums from the club a block away! Some folks boogied all the way to the entrance from their cars. Inside the smoke looked like it could smother the loud voices trying to talk through it and the music.

Dancers were swinging on the floor! Arms and legs flying. Colors of the dancers' clothes seemed to mesh in a kaleidoscope of design. I knew some of them: Wilma, Delbert, Delores and Richard, Kisha, Nisha, Romo, Domo, Nono, and Nomo were all out there with the others. Swinging away. Most didn't even come off the floor when the music stopped for a minute. Those that did just took a few sips of their drinks, snatched a few quick conversations, and ran back to catch the next beat! Looked good to me. The world rocking on its merry way. I wasn't in church now!

Now, some things I know about, I don't do. But, I don't care what you do. Do it if you want to. I have my own plans for myself.

Some people went outside to smoke a little pot. Some grabbed a quick puff in the restroom. Some other people were sniffing a little coke. I listen, so I know things. A few dealers were there; they came to hear the music too. They look just like everybody else, maybe a little better. They didn't look as dirty as their usual life is.

A few pimps were there. Well, social life is social life. They were alone; I guess their working women were on some corner or other. The pimps circulated around, whispering sweet somethings in somebody's ears. I saw their eyes flash as they looked over some women's shoulders, checking around for the next woman they would talk to. After all, according to my mama, they had a car note due or needed a new suit and had a loan made at the gambling house they had to pay back. So, they were playing, but they were working too.

But it did look like everybody was having big fun. I danced until I dropped. I was already tired; we had been running all day, and it was after one o'clock in the morning! My cousin is invited to just about everything and I get to go! So I found an empty seat in one of the booths way in the back. Where I could just look at people enjoying themselves, like a theatre of real life.

"The world is moving on its merry way! No one can halt it!" I smiled at the thought of my mama always saying that.

I watched the owner of the club, Shadow. He is a nice-looking macho man. I watched him listen to the cash register ringing to the music. I could see he was pleased. He had told everybody it was his birthday too! I wondered was it, or was it just to make somebody spend some money on a drink for him. I heard my cousin say he was always pulling that stuff cause it made some people buy a bottle of champagne for him.

At the moment, he was concentrating, looking over the pretty fly girls, to see which one he wanted to give him his special present tonight. His woman was at his house taking care of their two illegitimate children. He wouldn't marry her.

I listen, chile. My mama always tellin me to "shut my mouth and listen"!

I had danced so much I was just about exhausted. So I leaned back a little, resting my head, and curled my legs up under me. Suddenly I heard Shadow announce he had an unusual idea. I opened my eyes as he said, "A after-party! We are going to party hardy!" He looked around the rooms as he moved through the crowd, telling his closer friends to "stick around" after the club closed. For the after-party. Then he must'a found his "man," a dealer; he led some fellow over near the booth I was laying in. I heard him order some cocaine, on credit. He said, "I think I had a good night at the cash register."

The dealer asked him how much pot he wanted. Shadow said, "Not too much cause that shit just put some people to sleep." I had to smile to myself, cause I was already sleepy. Then he told him, "It better be good, man!"

The man answered, "It always is!" Then Shadow went back to listen to his cash register ring. And you could tell by the expression of glee on his face he was eagerly looking forward to the end of this part of the night.

I searched the crowd with my eyes, to see how my cousin was doing, cause I know it's about time for us to leave. We both have to go to work in the morning. She still having a good time and it's not two o'clock yet, so I don't bother her. I lean back on the seat and close my eyes. To listen to the music, you know?

Chile, even with all that noise, I fell asleep.

I woke up, slowly, to soft, steady noises. I must have slept a long time because the musicians were gone and the jukebox was playing. The lights were even lower than they were when the club was open. But in the shadows of light there were twenty or twenty-five people scattered randomly through the room.

Shadow still had a man serving drinks, much stronger drinks than they had served earlier in the night. He kept watch over a dish of something near him that he and two or three other people were dipping into.

Everyone seemed to be relaxed, laughing, and some of them were talking and pulling on each other. Shadow shouted to his guests, "Drink up! Let's really have a party!" Then he snapped his fingers at some girl that was sitting behind the bar near him. She got up and began to take her clothes off. He came from behind the bar, reached out for another woman, and swung her out for a slow step or two. Other people started to dance, close and slow. Others just kept getting high. Or whatever they were doing.

Shadow had a girl-friend or friend-girl, watching him closely. (Not his main woman, who was not there.) This girl was very young, she hadn't been there when the club was open. Shadow signaled to her, with a flick of his wrist, to dance or get out on the dance floor. She did what he told her; started dancing and even taking her clothes off! (I found out later, from my cousin, that these girls always did what he told them to do, for the drugs.)

Some men settled in a little closer to watch and began goading the other women to compete with her. "Show your fine body, baby! Awww, you ain't bashful, are you? Get on out there and show your own movie-star stuff! You look good to me with your clothes on, so I know you look good with your clothes off! Go on, girl!" Some women took another drink and, laughing, did what the men asked.

Soon, the floor was full of naked bodies! I was mesmerized. I hadn't made any noise and I was way back in the dark. I tried to see if I could find my cousin, but I couldn't see good enough.

Shadow was walking around with his little saucer and a something, maybe a little spoon or something, feeding the noses of the women. The bartender was pouring drinks aplenty and the jukebox didn't need any money put into it, it just kept playing real low bluesy music.

In another half hour most all the women were naked or down to their drawers, or thongs. Men were saying nice things about their bodies, persuading them to go even further. I knew I needed to go, get out of there, but I couldn't close my mouth or move my feet.

Then Shadow dared a fellow to have sex with his girlfriend

who lay on the dance floor on her back, dancing, spread-eagled! I know she must'a been high on drugs.

Wasn't long to wait; a macho-man took the dare and removed the last few pieces of his clothes, gladly, and went to work on the stretched-out lady. She knew how to moan, and soon there were other moans in corners of the room: in booths, under tables, and everywhere. Shadow among them. He had chosen his targets early because, when I had been dancing I had seen him staring at this woman, shoving drinks at her.

After a short time, Shadow called out, "Switch! Next! Oh, Lawd, this woman got me going!" He didn't change his partner, though. But almost everybody else did.

Most people didn't seem to question the command, they just took on the next partner. Some women got up and looked for somebody they wanted. A few women tried to say no, one was enough, but they were talked down or someone crawled up their legs with a tongue. People were even sucking on toes and fingers! They were licking and poking, sucking and (I could make a rhyme). It looked like a big pot of stewed, boiling oxtails. Have mercy! I have never seen, nor dreamed I'd see, anything like that. And I am not a virgin. I know a little about life. I thought.

I am a listener, but I am a watcher, too.

I figured it was time for me to get out of there before someone discovered me back up there in the dark. I hadn't seen my cousin, but I had seen a lady and a couple of fellows who had been at church this morning. I looked around for a place or way to get out. But I would have to go through the crowd! Lordy!

I didn't see the drugs being passed around anymore and the bartender was no longer behind the bar. It was empty back there. Some people were even looking for their clothes: a slip here, a brassiere there, some boxer shorts over somewhere else. Clothes all mixed together in a pile with sweatshirts and things. I can see!

It looked like some people were avoiding looking at other people. There was less laughter now, but still, some. I knelt down to the floor. I could still see them, but I crawled, slowly, toward what must be Shadow's office, cause I knew there must be an exit door around there somewhere. There was! It was locked, but the key was in it. I turned it and fairly flew through that door.

Outside there was a woman trying to start her car. Two men, who musta been in her most intimate business a few minutes ago, said they didn't have time right then to help her. They had to get home because their old ladies, etc., etc.

Other people were straggling out the front of the club and I could hear Shadow calling after them, "You bastards sucked up all my coke!" But he wasn't sounding really mad. I guess that's what he bought it for, and he had gotten his hands on, at least, two of the women he wanted. I observe, honey!

But, right then, I needed a ride. I called my cousin Lucy from the outside telephone booth. She answered the phone sleepily. I told her I needed a ride. She said, "Ain't you here? At home? I thought you musta got in the other car and they had dropped you off here."

"Well, I ain't, I didn't, and I'm not! Will someone please

come get me? I have to get up in three hours to get to the clinic for my job." She came and I rode home telling her everything that I had seen.

I listen. I watch. And I talk.

I rushed to bed, but I couldn't fall asleep. I showered and went to my job.

The events of the party were roiling around in my brain that morning as I consulted with the patients who needed psychiatric referrals and gave a few shots and brochures out. Then one of the men who had been at the party came in. I recognized him! He talked to one of the nurses.

He had had a bout with his guilty conscience and had come in to tell about the party he had attended. Because he had an STD, gonorrhea, and had been pretty busy at the party, AND didn't want the people, his friends (?), to not know what they probably had, and spread it around. Now! Soon there was a lot of "to do" in the clinic, which ended with two of the social workers leaving. Then . . . I'll tell you what I think happened.

The party people went home, showered, and were sleeping it all off. At about ten o'clock that morning someone rang bells, or knocked on doors, awakening the sleepers and their spouses or whatever. The caller was someone from the city's health department to explain to them what had happened. They were to report, immediately, to the clinic for examination and treatment and report.

They had to get up and go report in. Right now! My, my.

Everyone at the orgy, whose address the health department could find right away, met again. Far sooner than they would have wanted. They had thought their night was over, but that night was going to last a long time, chile.

One man and one woman had even gone home and "made love" (?) to their spouses, or whatever. Perhaps because the orgy had not satisfied them? It was a chaotic mess.

Well ... the party really was over. Even a few church members had to come in. I reflected that their minister did not really preach good enough. He tickled their ears; he didn't slap their minds with the truth. And some self-respect. Sometimes you don't have to wait to go to hell to pay for your sins. You can pay for some right here on earth!

They skulked in, heads lowered into the collars of their coats.

They all sat on the bare wooden benches against the army green walls, and looked up, looked down, looked across, looked just anywhere, but in someone's face and eyes. They were ashamed, disgusted, and embarrassed. Everyone was remembering when somebody's legs were back over their shoulders; when somebody's head had bobbed between their thighs, male and female, and where their own head had been. I would bet they all wondered who had had the disease and cursed the person, soundly, in their minds.

And! With all the blood tests and slides, three people in the group had herpes, one had gonorrhea, and one had syphilis!! And they still had to wait for the results of the HIV tests. They sure couldn't be taking care of themselves! And they didn't even look like the kind of people you would think had all these problems! But, what kind of people go to such a party anyway?

I may stay celibate the rest of my life. But, I hope not; I want a husband. My own man.

Finally they were through with the whole process and were leaving with their next appointments made already. They left the clinic, rushing swiftly to their cars, and drove away. Hurrying someplace where there were no eyes to see them. Some to sleep. Some to argue and fight, I bet.

Yeah, the party was over. Some friendships were gone. My cousin Lucy said it took a long, long time for some of them to go back to the club again.

But those are not all the important things. Even now, some people did not think of the party as a cunning, ruthless, hypocritical, lying thing to do. I think there were a few young, and yeah, innocent women and men there, that hadn't come there with nothing on their minds but dancing. There are still some innocent people in this world. Very few. But that party, a kind of drugged-up mess, is one of the reasons why I'm proud my cousin did not stay for the "after-party."

That "Soul" people love to say they have can get messed up if you don't think about which world you want to live in, and who rules it. You can degrade your own dignity, and respect may be gone. Forever. You get one life. Whose hands you put your life in and how you use it up is important. God said so. Satan is alive and well! And if your minister ain't tellin you something real, they ain't tellin you nothing!

Anyway the party is over.

I know you want me to hush. I will.

But my mama told me I better always try to know what is going on in my life. I told you, I listen to my mama.

I watch, I listen. And I talk. I tell it all, chile!

Catch a Falling Heart

When anybody is born, at that minute, that's the last step you get in life that was known and expected. No one ever knows what the next step is going to be. You can hope, but you can't know. Things start happening to some people before they are even able to think and make choices for theirself. Later, when they're older, some people don't even know they have choices so they just go any which way life casts them. Takes thinking, and it don't look like there is too much thinking around. I feel dumb myself, sometimes; a lot.

Sometimes you are handed a plate of life and, if you are poor, there ain't too many good choices on the plate. Some things look good, but they ain't. And some choices are hidden under something else on that plate.

People think rich people don't have to worry, that their life is taken care of, but that ain't true. Cause life ain't worth living if you don't have something valuable in it, besides money, for your spirit. That's why some people be rich and miserable as any other fool who thinks more money will make their life better. It won't. Money don't feed the spirit. Money may buy you a little lust; what you get for greed, sometimes, or envy. But money won't buy you love. Money may fill your eyes and your hands, but it won't fill your heart and spirit.

Rich people commit suicide, too. Like any other miserable person.

These kids committing suicide today? This world is feeding them poo-poo and telling em it's good for em. That it's all they need. But it don't feed their spirit. Their spirit grieves.

All this dope millions of people take today? What they trying to get? Where they trying to go? Out of emptiness into emptiness.

Another thing, plenty people spend millions and millions of dollars, and their whole life, trying to prove to people that God does not exist. They're lying. And, why would they spend their life, and their money, trying to help you? Keep you from believing in God? Why they want you to starve your spirit?

God feeds the spirit. Love feeds the spirit. Your spirit feeds your life. There ain't too much of God and Love in this world. I don't care how many people are lying about it. Takes thinking to live life. Thinking.

Well, that's enough of that because I'm not a preacher.

What I was telling you about things being on your plate of life when you are born is what I was thinking about this morning.

Thinking about a woman in this town I have known since she was a child, Harriet.

This ain't no big town, but it don't have to be. Things happen here just like they do everywhere else in the world cause people is people, don't care what color they are or where they are born. We got a body of water here, piece of the ocean, that brings a lot of port business and sea-people. A whole lot of business goes on in this place. All kinds.

I don't live far from the busy section of the coast and right down the street from me is a rooming house that stands for the Oceanview Hotel. Long ago, when this was just a middlin-poor section of town, that "hotel" used to belong to my husband's friends, Jefferson and Matilda Long.

Jefferson owned it. He was a sailor when he won the rooming house at the gambling table. He was not too clean, with a real dirty mouth. He was old by the time they married. Matilda was bout the only one who would marry him. Matilda was from a real, real, poor, poor family and wasn't too good-lookin herself. That's probably why she married him; wasn't much on her plate, you see.

They staggered into each other one night at the Water's End Bar, got happy, and got married. That old man could still make babies, though. I really believe they was his. She was so happy to be married and be taken care of, even if she had to do all the work. I don't believe she cheated on him. They had two children, Harriet and Star. Fine girls, when they was born.

Some years passed and he died first, cirrhosis of the liver.

Scared Matilda and she didn't go over there, to the bar, to drink so regular. She stayed home and ran the business and took care of her children. She was a good mother for a long time.

The hotel was a good business because it sits right across the street from the Water's End Bar. Young and old, seamen, business-men, prostitutes, and some ladies and a preacher or two went there. People staggering out late at night came straight across the street to get a room. So it was a good business.

Ships always coming in or going out. My husband used to go to the Water's End Bar. Sometimes I'd go with him because I like to see things, watch people, and look at life going on around me. The bar stayed busy. They hated to have to close sometimes, but they did have to.

Them girls, Harriet and Star, were nice-looking girls, but Star was the best looking when they were young. And fast, she was the spoiled baby. When they got older, in their teens, Harriet was the best looking. She was also sweet, which I think made her pretty. Star was arrogant and mean and selfish. She didn't like to do her share of work either.

You know, it ain't too many pretty people in this world, that's why them people who make face-paint make so much money. People can make a new face for themself. A new one every day, do they want to.

Anyway, while the girls were in their teens, Harriet was fool-ing around up on the garage one day, and fell off. That fall messed with her back and she still can't stand up straight no more ever. And something in her nervous system causes her body to shake real hard whenever she gets excited or angry, otherwise she is fine. Still, she is the naturally prettiest one, such as she is. Star is pretty with that paint working for her.

The years passed and Matilda forgot about her husband, Jefferson, dying from the liver trouble. Her memories of "good times" and loneliness got the best of her mind. She thought her plate was empty. She slowly began moseying cross that street again. To the Water's End Bar. She forgot about the full plate right there within her business and her children. It wasn't too long before the liquor ate up the rest of that poor woman's body and, then her plate really was empty.

But Matilda had taught the girls well, and had even put a little money by. In the months following her funeral Harriet had to take over the business. It just naturally fell to her. She had dropped out of school earlier because of her accident. She didn't like to take a chance on shaking in front of everybody, but, still, she was smart.

Harriet didn't like to go out of her hotel-home for nothing. But Star was always gone. So, naturally, Harriet finally was the one who did all the paperwork and everything else. Star treated Harriet like she was her employee or an old woman without no possibility for a life.

Harriet hired a lady, Ms. Poker, to change the beds, see to the clean linen, and vacumn every week. She kept the business working for the money they both needed. That house wasn't making no fortune cause they couldn't charge much. What it mostly was to people was a quick convenience.

Star couldn't do any work, for long, sitting at that desk that sat in the front window looking directly at the Water's End Bar. She loved watching all the goings-on round the bar; looking and laughing at the people. She would tell Harriet, "Pay somebody to watch this ole piece of junk! I ain't got time to do this mess! I'm too young to be stuck inside this place all the time! I ain't dead and I ain't shaking round ugly all the time." Star loved Harriet, but in her own selfish way.

But Star would put her hand in the till and take what money she needed when she needed it. She always found some there. So.

Ms. Poker watched the young women a while as she did her own thinking. Soon she stopped Star, a little, without her knowing it. Ms. Poker took a old cigar box and, every time she passed through the office with her dustin rags, she took half the money out of the cash register whenever she knew some money was there. She would put it away until she could give it to Harriet later. She thought to herself, "I got to see that she got money to pay me, cause I need my money." Harriet was grateful because she thought she shouldn't treat her sister, Star, that way. Huh!

The most money came from renting the three rooms set aside for prostitutes for twenty minutes at a time. A few rooms were rented to a couple of old-timers on a steady basis. The rest were rented to sailors who were unable to make it back to the ship. Very seldom, if ever, did the townspeople rent a room.

Another thing Harriet had learned in school was how to sew. So that filled in some of her time. In the beginning she had planned to make pretty clothes for herself, but she began to make dresses for the townspeople and mend pants and things for the men. She would sit in the front window to sew. It broke the monotony. Always in that window, she could look out, seeing who was coming and going at that bar.

It's pretty busy, if you know waterfront life. These people love to drink and party like tomorrow may not be coming. She used to see her mother over there, but now she saw Star. I'm talking years.

I used to go over there to that bar, more when my husband was alive than I ever would go now. I notice that no matter how long, no matter who has done gone and ain't coming back, and whoever is new and just started coming, they all look alike. The new women begin to look like the ones who left. They all laugh all the time, same empty loud laughter. They mostly all need to see a dentist. And after a while they don't look healthy. Maybe it's just me, but that's what I think. All that darkness and smoke and lying just steal into your skin.

Star, too! I told you she could make herself pretty. When she was younger you'd see her round, pretty face in there tween them grey, homely, and used ones. She became a regular regular. Oh, it takes a little time, just like age, but every day something's happening, changing you. Course, you throw some alcohol on top of that, cheap or expensive, it happens faster.

Over the years, yes, years, it happened to Star. Bar too close. She couldn't come out of her house without that bar beckoning to her. She would run in for a few minutes and stay a few hours. Too many men talkin sweet to her. Telling her lies they had picked up from places all around the world. Some men she got to know was nice, but they mostly belonged to somebody else at home.

Now Harriet looked out that window, too! She saw what looked like fun to her. But she did not dare to let herself out for everyone to really see. She wanted that desk counter to hide her. She'd go to the store or something, shop for material cause she didn't mind the townspeople, who had known her all her life, seeing her. It was strangers who would never know how she had been when she was young, who bothered her.

Harriet could hear that music blasting and all the revelry going on in that bar at all hours till three or four o'clock in the morning when it closed. She longed, I know!, she yearned to go over there and meet some of them men and make a new friend. Must'a dreamed of how they might fall in love with each other. She wanted to have love.... Well, who don't? with any sense! Love and God is what life is all about. She went to church every Sunday. But she was too scared and shamed to go cross that street to that bar. So, through the years she grew older, watching the bar doors open and close, looking and pretending she might see a man for her own.

Through the years, now and again, Star brought a man home. Well, she was young and pretty. One time one of her loves wanted to marry her and take her away, to home, with him. She thought someone better might be on the next ship, so she stayed, waiting, to see. Then a man might stay with her a day or two, or keep her awhile longer. But she was so selfish and mean, she couldn't keep a future planned with them.

She thought she had found true love a few times. And was happy, a few times, I guess. I think she gave up a lot for such empty happiness. Life will lie to you! Specially if you already lying to yourself! She was hoeing her row and raking in the wrong garden.

Star was no whore, she didn't charge a dime. So pretty soon, you know the prostitutes didn't like her no more for stealing their business. So they took to lying about her, to whatever man she was getting close to, so she couldn't keep him. Or he didn't want to keep her. Finally, time came when no one asked her for her little soft, growing ugly, hand in marriage anymore.

Star never did look back over her shoulder and think about her sister being lonely in that house all the time by herself with only Ms. Poker for company. Star never did look around and think about anybody, but herself. She needed that money from the hotel, though. In some clear moments, she thought about, and bought vitamins for Harriet. To keep her well and working. Harriet already slept well, she and Ms Poker ate well. So Harriet was healthy and strong.

Now . . . I happen to believe every Cinderella has got a Prince somewhere.

I sit on my porch a lot, and watch the world go by myself. I go down there and visit with Harriet when I need a little change of scenery and, also, because I sincerely care about her. Sometimes

I have something I want sewn. And I like to talk to her. Most time I just sit at home and read. I belong to a book club.

Over time, one day there was a middle-age man, named Issy Evers, who came to my house for one of my rooms. Almost everybody close to the port will rent a room out now and then. He worked as a cook on one of them ships. Fair-looking man with a few grey hairs mingled with the brown. Must'a been about thirty-nine or forty years old.

It was plain to see Mr. Evers had a back problem that gave him a gimp leg that made him seem kind of crippled. Least he couldn't walk smooth and sexy like some of his shipmates. His back was bent a little, real rounded of his shoulders. He was shaped like a slender "S." His hips pressed forward. He couldn't move his back from side to side, he had to take a whole step, not lean over sideways. But he didn't act crippled. And he worked!

I saw loneliness printed on his face, mostly in his sad, unexpectant, eyes.

I let him stay at my house one time, so I could see what kind of man he might be. I learned he had been to prison for something he didn't do. He was working on the ships to stay away from crooked police. And probably cause he didn't have no other home. I asked him about his wife. He quietly laughed, and looked at me like I was confused or something. Then he said he didn't have none.

I told him, "You can't bring any women here to my house, son. I don't 'llow that. This is a clean, safe house."

He gave me that same look again. Said, "I respect you, lady."

I told him my name. "Ms. Realer, son." I could have said "Mrs.," but that takes too long to say. I like "Ms." cause it's quick and easy.

He nodded his head and said, "If you need to know, it's been a long time since I put myself in that position. I had a woman, but she died two years ago with cancer. She understood me. I took care of her." He lowered his eyes a moment. Then he said, "There's too much sh . . . stuff out there now. You can't be sure no more. And I don't like people, women, thinking they are doing me a favor. I'm a grown man. If I ever just really have to, I'll wait till I get somewhere I know. Does that settle your mind, Ms. Realer?"

"Yes, sir, Mr. Evers." He stayed at my house four days and I enjoyed his silences, our talks, and his peace. He paid in advance for when he would return because his ship had a run that would stop here once a month for four or five days.

Emmh! Emmh! Emmh! It's sad for people to be without anybody in this crowded world. If there just wasn't so many fools in it, things would be way better for everybody; the fools too!

The next time he came to town and wanted a room from me, I had already decided I didn't want him staying at my house. I didn't give his money back. I lied, but I had to. I told him I had relatives coming in, but I knew just the place for him and had already reserved, and paid for, a room for him. Then I took him down to the Oceanview Hotel, and introduced him to Harriet. Told her, "This is the good man I gave you the money for to reserve one of your rooms."

I turned to Issy (that's what I had come to call him when he stayed at my house). Said, "Mr. Evers, this is Miss Harriet Long. This is a good hotel. Safe." Star wrinkled my mind a minute, but I threw the thought out. "I think you will be comfortable here. They gonna feed you, too, good food, so you don't have to eat at the greasy-spoon cross the street." I knew he wasn't interested in going over there anyway; he had already passed it up once.

Since then, Mr. Evers always rented a room at Oceanview. Said he was tired of viewing the ocean, but, "Your hotel is nice and homey, Ms. Harriet." That's what he said to Harriet. I was there.

I forgot to tell you, Issy Evers didn't never hardly look nobody in the face and eyes either. I think he thought he was ugly, well, he kind'a was. Had a scar cross his face from trying to keep somebody from raping him when he was in prison. Stay out of prison if you have to use everything in your brain you can, cause life ain't never the same, I don't b'lieve.

Now, I didn't have no reason or anything for taking him down there, just sometimes your heart tells you to do something. I didn't need his money. Lord knows, I'm old and I got enough. It ain't no million dollars or nothing near that, but how much does a person need? You can't spend it all. That Solomon was right, life is a vanity. Spend all your life doing something like making money and you still got to leave it behind. Cause it can't buy you life. Besides, I pay attention to my heart; see how it's beatin and all, and hear what it's trying to tell me.

He didn't like lookin at people straight in the face and that desk was in front of Harriet. She didn't like people to see her body, I don't really know why; her body did not look crooked. Only she knew the shaking going on inside of her. They could'a passed each other by, just like that.

I told him, "You can come down and talk to Harriet just like you talked to me. She likes to read, too."

She smiled and frowned at the same time, but at least she smiled. She said, "Yes, come on down. I like to hear stories about the different places you have been. I haven't been anywhere." See, she didn't know him, so she thought she wouldn't get excited and shake in front of him. She continued, "We'll call you when your dinner is ready." She handed him the key. "You got a lucky room, number seven."

They must'a made friends cause Issy went back to the Oceanview Hotel every time his ship was in port. Sometimes he came by my house to see me.

I forgot about it because I have my own stuff to tend to. But I did drop in on Harriet when I had to pass by. We talk and I watch her fingers make the needle go in, go out, then the machine go up and down. All them stitches and probably one her dreams stuck in em. One time I went, she was making a wedding dress for someone. Someone else's dream with hers mixed in.

Once, when I was there, Star was going out, and Harriet told her sister, "Why don't you eat something before you go out? You need some food on your stomach. It's already cooked, you just need to warm it up and eat it."

Star looked at me and smiled (she knew her sister loved her

and it's so good to be loved). She went out the door, saying, "She don't ever go nowhere, Ms. Realer. She's going to let her shakes hold her down. I told her, life is going to pass you by. But not me! I'm going to get me some life!" She went flying after life like a bird, but never got any farther than across the street. And seem to always come home with her feet draggin.

Well, anyway . . .

Sometimes, if it was evening, me and Harriet would have a little drink. Yes! We drank brandy. Not a lot, just a little. She like to serve it in them little snifters she had bought to go with her romantic dreams. (I know she had em, I think everybody does.)

One time, when we were having a drink, Harriet said to me, "My days go by like hours of sand. Lots of hours. Lots of sand." Then she stopped talking because Star came in.

Star greeted me and told Harriet, "You ain't gonna offer me a drink? Just gonna sit up here with Ms. Realer and leave me out!? I am family, and friend, ain't I?"

Harriet went to get a glass for her. Star called after her, "Don't get me one of them baby glasses either. Give me a grown-up glass." But Harriet brought her a snifter anyway.

I took a good look at Star. The children I had known as babies were older now. Certainly. But the years seem to bite and chew up Star's face; I don't mean it was a ragged, scarred face, it just looked too used. Like a plastic doll some child had loved and banged around so long, until even the doll looked . . . broken and worn, is all I can say.

Her face was beginning to crease, and dry them creases in

place. Not a soft wrinkle, but a crease. In a puffy face that still held some attraction, you could see what once was there. She was thirty-five or thirty-six, younger than Harriet by a year, I b'lieve.

I smiled into her eyes. I cared about her, just thought she didn't care enough about herself. As she laughed with us, no matter how she tried that empty laughter, if you watched real close you could see the tears sittin in the corner of her eye. Emmmh! Emh! All them men . . . and she still lonely. She thought she was getting love, but it dried up before the sun could hit it. The quivering sighs, the blissful moans, couldn't outstrip the broken promises, the lies and a couple of times, a black eye.

Well, that's Star. She is doin what she think is best for her, I guess. Or what she saw her mother do. Get you some education about what is going on in this world. See what's going on besides what's across the street. This is a big world! And I don't care what they say about them computers, you can't live in one of em!

I told you someone had asked Harriet to make a wedding gown. It was some beautiful white satin. They must'a stole it because you could tell it was expensive, soft and full-bodied, fit for a queen. It looked like it could caress and kiss the skin it touched. Then the wedding must didn't go on like it was supposed to, and they didn't want the dress. Least they didn't never come get it. It hung on Harriet's rack for about two years. Harriet kept it clean and dust free.

She loved to look at that dress and touch it with her soft, gentle hands. Her needle finger was the only thing that snagged it. After a time, Harriet began to speak of it as hers. Well, it was; she hadn't been paid for it. Finally she took some of that dress loose and fixed it to fit her own body. Some nights, in her room alone after her work, she would try it on. Careful, careful not to muss it. I saw it, it fell softly and rich on her slightly bent body, and her back liked to straightened out. She felt like the sun or a star in that dress. Like a cloud of beauty.

It was her dream. It was her secret shared only with me. Because there was no groom, you see. She knew Star would have laughed at her; maybe affectionately, but a laugh at ya is a laugh at ya! During this time . . . Star had started sneaking men in the hotel late at night. For money. The prostitutes had convinced her she was a fool for giving it away. They wanted to see her come to be a regular whole whore. Misery really do like company. Well, I don't think Star was no whore at heart because she didn't do it often. But she did do it sometimes.

Ms. Poker knew it first, but it didn't take long for Harriet to find out. She didn't say anything to her sister because she took care of Star with the hotel money, and it was never enough. And because times were hard and sewing didn't pay much. And she was working on a new dream of her own.

Harriet had lived in the Oceanview Hotel all her life. Every day, every hour of her life. She wasn't dreaming of a real man, only an imaginary one. She was sure no real man would want her. But she was dreaming of a house of her own so she could move away from the Oceanview Hotel and the Water's End Bar.

She told me, "I can still come to work every day, but I want to be . . . more alone. To myself. Have a place that's just mine. Some peace. Maybe set up a real little shop for sewing. Make a better life for myself."

Harriet had been saving some of her money over the years. Her share after she shared the hotel income with Star, paid the bills, and Ms. Poker. She didn't do much more than work, so there you are. For the last ten or fifteen years she had put a little by, steady. She had learned that from her mother.

When I learned that, I set out looking for a little house for Harriet. Was fun to me; I like to do things out the usual, and every woman likes lookin at houses. I found something once or twice I thought she would like, then she would come out to see it. We finally found just the perfect little house for her. It was a ground-floor house with a nice-sized kitchen beside a closed-in porch, two bedrooms, a small dining room, and a living room. Had a picket-fenced-in yard big enough for a few large, strong trees already there, and room for a small garden for Harriet to plant her vegetables. She could even have another dream of hers: two chickens, hens. Two fresh eggs every day!

She put the money down on the house and told me, "Now I can have a nice dog and my cat won't be petted by strangers all day. Cleopatra [the cat] don't like that." We grinned at each other. She said, "I sure got to work hard sewing now, cause I got a house of my own to pay for!" Her eyes teared up when she said that. She was happy and she shook only a little.

Issy Evers came into port round that time, and went to the

Oceanview Hotel. He always did now, cause he and Harriet had made up a quiet friendship talkin about the world and books. This time in their little talks, she told him her secret about the little house. Well, it's all she could talk about. And it happened to be one of Issy's dreams too. But he had never thought it would come true. Too big a dream, to him. He just thought he would work until he died and he had insurance to bury himself and that would be that.

One day we were sitting and talking round Harriet's desk. She was talking about her having to work at her sewing harder to pay for the house. You know, like people do, not hinting, just stating facts. Issy must'a gave some thought to that. He asked, "You mean you might not be here much anymore?"

She smiled a little sadly. "Not any more than I have to, but I think I'm going to have to."

Then he said, "I won't be here but a few days; can I see your house, Ms. Harriet, please?"

Harriet tried to say no, but I was there and I said, "Sure." I smiled at both of them, said, "We going over there today, just in a little while. Come on back in a hour or so." Harriet squirmed and fidgeted, but she didn't want to start shaking, so she didn't say anything until he went to his room.

She meant to whisper, but she was agitated so it was loud. "Ms. Realer, why you want to tell him he can go with us? I don't want to be shaking round nobody. I don't shake around you cause I know you. And now, he's going to be there. I don't know him. He's just a nice stranger. Now, he's gonna see me shake."

I just told her, "Everybody is a stranger till you know em! He been coming here almost a year! And you told me he was a nice man and you liked him." I added, just for looks, "As a friend. He probably done already seen you shakin. So what?! What's a little shake? It's your shake, Harriet. So, so what?"

So we all went; I went with em. This homeless man with nothin but a room anywhere, looked like a hungry kitten as he looked around the yard and the little house. The kitchen had cleaning supplies left around from her steady cleaning work, and she had put a few of her things in some room every time she came.

She was foolin with something and he was just standing there watching her. I was standing there watching them. Finally he asked her, "Are you going to be livin alone here?"

I answered, "Well, yes. She is not married."

Harriet turned maroon as she said, "Yes, nobody but me is going to be living here."

He looked at me, then turned back to her. Said, "Well, Ms. Harriet, I'd like to ask you something. I don't intend to be fresh, or bad-mannered, and try to break in on your plans, but . . . Well, Harriet, I get so tired of hotels and rented rooms, and carryin all the things I love everywhere, and every time, I go. Could I, please, ask you to rent me that extra room of yours? By the year? I'll pay one hundred dollars a month. A year in advance. Just let me put my things in that room, and keep it empty . . . till I get here once a month for three or four days? I'm quiet. I'm clean. I know you like to be let alone; I won't bother you. Would you, please, think about it?"

Harriet was speechless. She did not want a rooming house in her home.

So I answered, "Why certainly, Mr. Issy Evers. Harriet would like that."

Harriet started shaking, so I told Issy, "You go on back, ahead of us. We'll be right along."

When he was gone, we both started talking at the same time. She said, "A stranger in here with me! No, mam!"

I said, "I told you, everybody is a stranger till you know em. Sides, that man is no stranger to you. He been a customer of yours for a long time and you always liked him before! Think about it, girl. That hundred dollars a month, paid in advance, for a person you will not see but three or four days out the month. You will have your house to yourself. And . . . you can almost retire, cause you have to sew aplenty for a hundred dollars a month." I could see her thinking about that.

She squinched her lips all the way back to the hotel, but she didn't say another word to me. And she wasn't shaking. She hugged me when we said good-bye, though. I smiled all the way home.

The next time Issy Evers came to town he moved into his room at Harriet's house. I smiled some more.

Well, bout another year went by. The first time Issy had come into town, Harriet had come over to my house to spend the night instead of staying at the hotel. Before she got that house, Issy had already started coming by to see me every time he came to town.

This time he looked worried. He frowned as he said, "Ms. Realer, I'm glad to have that room, but I don't want to run Harriet away from her own house. Maybe I could pay you to find some little house like that for me." We talked, but I didn't really say nothing.

The next time Issy came in town, I suggested to him that we all go out to dinner for some Chinese food. Harriet liked Chinese food and, since I was going to be with em, she relaxed. She went to eat dinner with us. She didn't shake. After that, she started staying at home. They went to different rooms, but they went to the same house.

After that first date, they started going out someplace, to have dinner or see a picture show, most nights he was in town. They went without me! Left me at home. (smile)

Harriet told me, "The prettiest things show up in the kitchen and the living room and my bedroom every time he comes to town. I got the most beautiful pictures on the walls. And, girl, he brings me the most beautiful material to sew things for myself with!"

I just smiled with her.

"I tell him to rest, after working all that time, but he won't! He works that garden and is making that chicken-house a little bigger and stronger so nothing can get in it . . . after our chickens, you know." (I heard that "our.") "We got four now. Issy said that's enough cause we don't need but four eggs a day and we don't always eat all of those. Besides, he likes to take me out so he can eat food he didn't cook. I don't let him cook for me either. Only sometimes, when he surprises me when I come home from work. But, I don't work on the days he is in town no more. Ms. Poker takes care of things; ain't that much to do noway." She took a breath and brushed an invisible something off her lap. Then, "You know his name is Isaiah, and that's why people call him Issy. When he's in town on a Sunday, we are going to start going to church with you. I'm going to start going with you more when he isn't here, too, Ms. Realer."

She just couldn't stop talkin, chile, tellin me how wonderful her life was. And I kept nodding my head, thrilled happy for her from my head all the way to my bottom sittin on that chair!

Now, I know about men, a little bit, pretty good. Issy was a nice man, a good man. And I have always liked men who have pushed-forward-lookin hips. (My husband was built that way.) I know what I'm talkin bout. I think. And I wanted something for my friend's starved life and heart. Sex ain't the most important thing in life, but if you're gonna have some, my friend Harriet deserved the best she could get. See what I mean?

And I knew she liked him, because she didn't shake much around him anyway. I didn't know how they would ever get to make love. I know sex is exciting, sometimes, and Harriet might get excited and start shaking. She wouldn't want him to see her shake. So how could they do anything? I didn't think they had ever got to that part of life yet. Sometimes you don't learn much sitting behind a desk, tryin to hide, for thirty years.

For the next two months, though, he had come in town and I hadn't heard a thing on those days, from either one of them. I hoped nothing was wrong. They are fun to be around. I always see her, but I missed him, too.

Now . . . I have a key to her house, you know, cause she lives alone most of the time. She has a key to my house for the same reason.

I got that key out of my drawer and sat down in a chair, thinking. I studied that key to Harriet's house a minute. Cause I ain't no meddling woman. But I need to know if my friend is all right. She didn't pass my house going to work, so . . . what are those two doing over there?

I got my coat and went walkin to Harriet's, since it ain't far. When I got there, I put the key in the lock, quietly, so I wouldn't disturb nobody.

The door opened without a squeak. I guess oiling hinges was one of the jobs Issy had been doing to that house. Keepin things in working order.

I reached the middle of the living room and stood stark still, and listened. And I could hear something.

I heard bed springs springing to a steady rhythm. I could hear a moan or two between them squeaking springs. I heard Issy say in a low, mellowed voice, "Shake, baby, shake." I heard Harriet's soft, happy laughter, a laughter mixed in with moans, that sounded sexy. I thought to myself, "He can only go up and down . . . and when she is excited, she shakes."

I backed up out of the living room, out the door, and went home. I was happy! For both of them, chile.

But I knew one thing that hadn't been settled.

I waited long enough for them to be finished, a couple hours, then I went back and rang the bell.

I said to them, because I am the oldest and I am involved, don't care what you think. I said to them, "I don't know what all is going on here, but I don't hear no wedding bells. I think it's time you thought of that."

Issy actually blushed, looking satisfied and happy. He said, "I got the ring; she just got to take it. I'm ready."

I looked at him and thought to myself, "I'll just bet you are."

I looked at her and she just blushed, looking down at her lap, laughing that sexy sound again. And she wasn't shaking. Too relaxed, I guess.

He took a month off of his job.

I gave the wedding at my house. Just a small one, people from the church and all like that. Star came, and brought a few of her friends. I could see some of them laughing, without sound, behind their hands. They were laughing at the mildly shaking woman in the beautiful satin, white wedding dress she had made with her own hands. They laughed a little at Issy as he stood stiffly, with his hand out, eagerly waiting for Harriet to walk to him.

Now, some of them didn't have husband or wife, no ring, no house, no real future, and, most important, no love. But . . . they had the nerve to laugh at some real people with real love.

They didn't laugh at that big diamond ring he put on her finger. And I saw the look Harriet gave Issy as they held hands. I saw the joy, the happiness, they gave each other. And they were going home to their *own* house that was full of their *own* love.

Sometimes, people say, for good luck, you have to catch a falling star and put it in your pocket. These two people, Issy and Harriet, had somethin better than good luck, they had a blessing. They had both caught a falling heart! And they were gonna take it home.

I looked life over as I was standing there, watching everybody. My plan had worked and two lonely, wonderful people were more happy. They were each other's life! It was always up to them. And I was happy too. I actually shook with my joy and laughter. Shaking, chile, shaking.